A Promise
to Papa

A Promise to Papa

LaJoyce Martin

A Promise to Papa

by LaJoyce Martin

© 2001, Word Aflame Press
Hazelwood, MO 63042-2299

Cover Design by Paul Povolni

Cover Art by Art Kirchoff

Printed in United States of America

Printed by

WORD AFLAME®PRESS
8855 DUNN ROAD
HAZELWOOD, MO 63042-2299

Library of Congress Cataloging-in-Publication Data

Martin, LaJoyce, 1937-
   A promise to papa / LaJoyce Martin.
      p. cm.
   ISBN 1-56722-582-9
   1. Frontier and pioneer life—Fiction. 2. Fathers—Death—Fiction. 3. Orphans—Fiction. 4. Girls—Fiction. I. Title.

PS3563.A72486 P7 2001
813'.54—dc 21
                                                    2001026737

Contents

The Story

"Nathalie . . ."

Nathan Thommason had few breaths left, and he couldn't afford to waste them. His last words must be spent on his only child, guiding and instructing her, for she would be left alone in an unfriendly township. Too honest, Nathan Thommason was, in glaring contrast with the corrupt city fathers. They hated both him and his daughter. He could not leave her to their mercy—or better said, their lack of mercy.

"Yes, Papa." The girl hurried to his side. "Can I get something for you? Broth? Water?"

"I . . . am . . . going, Nathalie," he rasped, each syllable costing great effort and subtracting from his waning supply of strength, "to join . . . your mother."

"No, Papa!" She clutched his hand as if to hold him in the land of the living. "Please don't leave me!"

"You will follow . . . my rules?"

"Oh, yes, Papa. Forever and always."

"Promise?"

"It is a promise!"

"You . . . must . . . go . . . west." The words were scarcely audible now, and his eyes took on the glaze of death.

"Where, Papa? Tell me where—"

But Nathan Thommason was gone.

Chapter One

Overheard Conversation

"I tell you, I'm agin it, Erman!" Larded with agitation, the brusque voice echoed from the gaming table at the back of the store. "We ain't takin' no unfamiliar lass along on the wagons. Is that clear?"

Pulse fluttering, Nathalie hid behind a pile of rank smelling furs. *They are talking about me!* she discerned. And she was right.

"I don't see why—" Erman argued.

"Why? Why?" A fist banged on wood—hard. "The girl ain't a wagon or funds to buy nothing. That's why! They say her paw left her with nothing. She would be a dead liability to us. Besides, she would prove herself a distraction to the menfolk. Mark my word. I know her kind."

"I'll find a family for her to fare with. There's some as would like help with the chores or a teacher for their children. I will pay her share of the cost. And I'll see that she isn't a problem to any man save myself. That's a pledge, Thaddeus."

"No, Erman, it won't work. Mark my word. Wives and younguns beget bad enough bother on the train, though I suppose they're an evil necessity. We won't be cartin' no extry skirts. The trip is long and tedious aplenty without askin' for troubles. You're wastin' your breath and my time with argumentations."

Nathalie hadn't moved, and—dishonorably, she knew—she was eavesdropping. Much ashamed, she fled the building, leaving the scent of leather and cheese and dry goods just uncrated. Once outside, she shivered, not because winter's nip still worried the air but because she was afraid.

The two men, who knew nothing of her coming or going, continued their conversation: "Then I won't pilot along with you," Erman stated decisively. "I will make up my own train and take the lass in my company. She no longer has a home here; I've been told she wishes to go west. And don't think I can't split up your party, Captain. Everyone knows that I have much more experience at caravans than yourself. Why, I could guide the outfit blindfolded! I have made the trip many times with few casualties."

Thaddeus narrowed his eyes; his whiskers dropped as he glowered. "Okay! Okay! Have it your way, Erman Whitt! We'll take her, but you will rue the day you made this foolish decision. Mark my word." (Thaddeus seemed to want all his words "marked.") He threw down the dominoes with a clatter and exited the store, his heels thudding noisily on the pine floor.

"Mad, is he?" The storekeeper raised his brows.

"He can get glad in the same boots that saw his mad," Erman said. "Wanting to leave behind an orphaned girl—"

"Don't know what all the 'going west' folly is about anyhow," groused the merchant. "There's a mania to it, if you ask me."

"I don't reckon we asked you."

"Same kind of folks here in Medford Mill, plenty to eat, and feathers to sleep on."

"You're talking to a man who hearts in the West, sir, where miles of virgin land await a plow and easy-to-get water calls. But best of all, it is venturesome. Real pioneer country. Easier laws. Beats sitting behind a counter with pickle barrels and calico. No fevers. Fresh opportunities. Elbow room."

"Each to his own. I'll take civilization. When is your train leaving?"

"Time is pushing. Nothing but the mud argues for a wait. Even with three-inch iron on the wheels, wagons have a hard run in mud. We're hoping to pull out by the end of the week."

With that, Erman hurried from the business, too. A heap of work needed to be done.

He would need to find the girl and let her know. . . .

Chapter Two

The Quandary

At her cabin, Nathalie collapsed into a sobbing heap on her bed, giving way to an avalanche of despair. *Where can I go? What will I do?* Panic singed her mind.

Crying wouldn't help a thing. It would only muss her face. But tears provide a woman with a spillway when her emotions can hold no more.

The trail boss didn't want her in his company—and with good reason. She had nothing to contribute, nothing with which to defray the trip's expenses. No money. No supplies. Why did she ever think she could join the wagons anyway? She was too proud to let a stranger pay her way. Nor would Papa approve. No, she decided, she would rather starve.

Was it just ten days ago that her father died, leaving her alone in the world? "You must go west, Nathalie," he whispered, the words but a thread of sound, tiny, thin, gasping, as he drew his dying breath. But "west" was a vast area, and he had not lived to tell her where to settle.

She must carry out his wishes, of course, though he hadn't been afforded the time to give her the reasons for his unusual request. Perhaps that was something he had wanted to do, planned to do, himself—to go west with the wagons. He hadn't been happy in Medford Mill. Without the buttress of friend or family, he stood alone in his integrity.

After his funeral, attended by few mourners, Nathalie reined her mind to rational thought. What was the rush to go west? She could wait a few months until she conquered her grief. Her familiar surroundings would be her solace. She had lodging and food for a while yet. A wagon train in town was preparing for departure, she'd heard, but she'd wait for a later one. Maybe next year . . .

Then, the week following her father's passing, the hammer fell. The banker, an unscrupulous vulture whose reputation didn't include advocacy for the less fortunate, hauled her to court and served her with an eviction notice. "Your father laid a heavy mortgage on his home," he said with cutting coldness. "I hold the lien. You will vacate the property by the end of the month. Take only your personal belongings. The furnishings are not to be removed. I have renters waiting to move in."

Nathalie had no idea how much her father owed, or if indeed he owed anything at all, but it mattered not. Little or much, she had no resources to make the payment. Nor had she the money to hire a lawyer, an agent who might prove as devious as the banker. She supposed that her father, giving no thought to the grim reaper, borrowed the funds for her schooling; he was adamant that she have a good education.

He planned, she knew, for her to be a teacher should

she be called upon to make her own way in life—but not at Medford Mill. The small town's schoolmarm, a timeless fixture, would be there forever. She was the banker's niece, the mayor's daughter, and the sheriff's sister. A new teacher was neither needed nor wanted.

Nathan Thommason hadn't been a popular man in the community. He had "bucked the system" on more than one occasion, standing in the gap for the poor against dishonest practices. Nathalie proudly shared in his ostracism. Thus, she was chagrined to learn that her father had left her vulnerable to their vagary. Death caught him, assisted by the hoof of a horse that brought internal hemorrhaging, before he outran the hounds of fate.

Now choice had been wrenched from Nathalie's hands. She had no one to stanchion her, to vouchsafe her property. Her father had been her sole mentor, her provider. She was left to "kill her own snakes" without a hoe. "You must go west" became more than a departing suggestion; it was an exigency.

Somewhere in California or Oregon or Washington or wherever "west" might be, there would surely be a colony desperate for a teacher who could read and write and could teach others to do so. To leave unpleasant memories, she considered, to go where Papa's vacant chair would not haunt her should prove a relief to her sore heart.

She was only nineteen; she could start over. Yes, her mind was settled. She must join this wagon train.

Then today, when she made inquiry at the general store about the caravan, the storekeeper informed her that she would need to talk to the trail boss. He didn't know the requirements, he said, or if they had their quota already. He was noncommittal, almost testy, but she did learn that the captain usually came in about four o'clock in the afternoon.

And she had returned to speak with him—only to learn that she was not welcome on the trip.

I'm not wanted. But I have no other option. I have no home. How would she solve this dilemma?

Tears spent—and with no answers—Nathalie fell into an exhausted sleep.

Chapter Three

Packing

A heavy knock jarred Nathalie from her dark nest of sleep. The banker? Had he come to drag her from the cottage into the street with derisive humor? A surge of sickness gripped her stomach. Raw fear built remorselessly to a crescendo that sent a bullet of terror up, down, and around her spine. Then it fragmented into searing shrapnel, becoming a ferocious pain with probing pinchers.

The knocking continued, and Nathalie commanded her body to respond. Passing the brown mirror, she caught her reflection in it, thinking wryly that she looked like a discarded doll, her dress rumpled and her hair askew. With one hand she smoothed her skirt, with the other, her hair. At the door, her hand trembled on the latch.

A man that she did not know stood on the stoop. He removed his hat in a gesture of acknowledgment. "Miss Thommason?"

"Yes?"

"We are making up a party to go west, Miss," he said

without preamble. "The Pascoe family from farther east is looking for a hired hand on their wagon. Only a woman will fit. The missus has a small baby and will need help with the trail work."

The man had crinkled dark hair, his eyes crowded under a low brow. Nathalie wouldn't have favored him with adjectives that befitted handsomeness, but neither was his appearance a thing to turn away.

Her mind harked back to the conversation in the mercantile. This was Erman; she recognized the voice. But, of course, he didn't know she had heard the argument in the store.

An aberrant coldness seized her. "I dare say the trail boss doesn't want an 'unfamiliar' lass along on the wagons," she said. "I'd be a liability. My father left me penniless. Besides, I might prove myself a distraction."

Erman stared at the toes of his boots so that his eyes did not meet hers. At once she realized he was the sort of man who could not give all his attention to what was at hand; part of him was somewhere else, looking backward or forward.

After a pause, he threw back his head and laughed, an indistinguishable kind of laugh that might mask pleasure or displeasure. "I see that the storekeeper has been talking to you," he said, "and I'm not surprised. He thinks that we are all daft for wanting to leave his beloved Medford Mill anyhow."

"Why, no," Nathalie answered. "The storekeeper said nothing to me. I haven't even discussed the matter with him."

"Well, never mind what the captain thinks or says, Miss Thommason. He is a fretful man. He would find something to fault each of us with if he could. That's his way. He means no harm, I'm sure. I am second in command, and if I say that you can go along on the wagons, you can go. And I say that you can go." He focused his eyes on her face, and there his scrutiny lingered. Then his glance measured the rest of her.

"I won't have a stranger paying my fare."

"There's no free ride, Miss. You will earn your way with work aplenty. However, if you don't want to go, we can fill your place. Easily. I have others begging space, but the choice is yours first."

Something itched and worried far back in Nathalie's mind. She wished she had not heard the converse in the store; her decision would be easier.

"The West offers great opportunities, Ma'am. You are young and strong. Don't waste yourself in this low, boggy country. In the West the air is dry and there's no fear of the fever. You really ought to give your word right now."

The man was almost . . . pushing. But why? Others, paying passengers, were waiting. Why was she given preference?

"I . . . I'd like to pray about it."

"Make it a hurried prayer then. We will be leaving before the week turns."

"What . . . what should I take? In the way of personal belongings, I mean?"

"There will be room for only one trunk, Ma'am. Space is very limited. If you have a wedding dress, take that. Most folks that go west don't ever wish to return once they've seen its beauty. You must go looking to the future."

"I'd have no reason to return. I have no one . . . here."

19

"Exactly. A better life awaits you."

Whatever her fate, could it be worse than the stagnation of Medford Mill? And where would she live if she stayed? Better death than the disgrace of serving in the alehouse for her room and board. She could never desecrate Papa's honor with such questionable employment.

"I'll go," she blurted and then desperately wanted to retrieve the words, though the reason for her wanting to do so was not clear.

"A wise decision." The man's busy eyes smiled their satisfaction. They rather glowed, Nathalie decided. "Best you begin your packing today, Miss. Two more days of friendly sun and soft spring winds will put us on our way to the land of enchantment." He clapped his hat on his head, mounted a black horse that stood ground tied in the yard, and was gone.

If the caravan planned departure in two days, Nathalie had no time to lose. Every moment counted. The preparation would motivate her, give purpose to her existence. She hastened her steps.

But as she reentered the house, trouble trounced her mind. Why did she feel uneasy? Was it the man, the trip, or her own unfounded fears that invited the inner turmoil? She hadn't time to peel away the layers of misgivings to find the core of the problem.

She had no trunk, but Papa had built a quilt box of white oak. That would have to suffice; she hoped it was not too large. Two quilts would fit in its cavernous body as well as her personal effects. She would use every inch to its best advantage.

A riptide of sadness crashed over her tired body, pressing her into her father's chair. This was the only home she had ever known. She had started building her world here as far back as her mind could stretch. Under this roof, her memories lived: hands clasped in prayer, the crackle of the fireplace, and the sound of Papa's deep chuckle. This house had recorded her own birth, the death of her mother and a baby brother. Each stick and splinter of the building was put there by Nathan Thommason's hands, and each touch of beauty paid tribute to her deceased mother. To leave the past would not be easy. But Nathalie reminded herself she had no alternative.

A pang of hunger tattled that she had eaten nothing all day. Food held no appeal for her, yet she needed nourishment. For a trip of unknown duration or destination, she had to be strong. A skillet of hominy grits rested against the stovepipe for warmth, and she filled her stomach with these, heedless of their delectable parched corn taste. Survival, not enjoyment, dictated her world now.

After the meal, Nathalie started to pack. Practicality prevailed. In the box went the two heaviest quilts, usurping the space for the lighter, prettier ones with their intricate patterns. Beauty didn't protect one from the cold.

For each of her loved ones, she gathered one small memoir. A china doll that had been her mother's had a corner, along with a tiny dressing gown made for her baby brother. Papa's Bible would be her sole keepsake on his behalf. These she stowed first before she folded her own garments.

If you have a wedding dress, take that. Why had the man mentioned a wedding dress? But, of course, he supposed that, being as young as she was, she would eventually marry. A fancy dress might be hard to come by in a remote area. She could take her mother's wedding dress, a simple chemise of ecru silk. It would suffice for her modest nuptials. This she laid carefully atop the quilts.

She supposed that she would marry in time, if ever she found an honest man. A man like Papa. But that wouldn't happen any time soon.

Her hands worked while her mind mulled. Extra stockings, a poke bonnet, and petticoats took more room than she anticipated; the container was filling quickly. But even at the sacrifice of some wardrobe items, she must find room for a calendar and her certificate from school.

In a tin bucket she put her hairbrush, a chunk of lye soap, a mirror, a needle and thread, and a rag. Was there anything else—?

What if the wagon train should run short of food? So frightening was the thought that Nathalie threw every item from the box and lined the bottom with the rabbit jerky her father had made. Then, not yet free of anxiety, she covered the meat with a layer of dried apples, including a canister of nutmeats her father shelled during the winter. Now, one of the large quilts would have to stay behind. She replaced everything but the quilt, packing her extra dress last.

For a long minute she looked about the room, wanting more than anything to put back into its place every article she had packed into the oaken chest. Almost . . . almost she changed her mind about going at all.

Then her father's final words came echoing back: "You must go west, Nathalie."

She had made a promise to Papa. She would keep that promise.

Chapter Four

On the Way

At daylight on Thursday morning, a canvas-shrouded schooner came to fetch Nathalie and her trunk. "Is that all you've got?" asked the driver when he saw the solitary quilt box.

"I . . . yes. That is, I didn't know there would be room for more."

"We have a larger wagon than most," the man, who introduced himself as Albert Pascoe, said. Albert, dressed in old buckskin breeches and a red checkered shirt, had a good face, intelligent eyes, a high forehead, and a grin that put one at ease immediately.

"You'd best throw in your feather ticking," he said. "A woman's bones aren't made to sleep on wagon floors. The feathers will make a comfort for sitting, too. And aren't you taking a pillow—?"

Nathalie shook her head. She didn't know whether or not her pillow and mattress would constitute "furniture" (which the banker had strictly forbidden her to take). She didn't suppose, though, that the self-preserving money lender would bother to pursue a wagon train for such trivial trappings.

Without waiting for her answer, Albert hauled the mattress from the bed. "And take the nice quilts, too, in case you don't come back. You'll find time to pine for covers if you abandon them. And we can tie that good chair there on the outside."

"Maybe I shouldn't—"

"Yes, you should," he said, taking matters into his own hands. "You will regret it if you don't."

The thought of taking Papa's chair consoled Nathalie. Could this be God's way of showing her that she had made the proper decision? Her mind grasped for a confirmation.

Albert's dogs sniffed and barked at the quilt box sitting on the porch. "Git, dogs!" scolded Albert, pushing aside the animals that followed the box, their noses pressed against it, the entire way to the wagon. "Well, bless my soul, I've never seen dogs so crazy over a trunk!" puzzled the man.

They smell my jerky! Nathalie's mind supplied. *I shouldn't have tried to take it.*

As Albert loaded, Nathalie took a last long look that would be her goodbye, bidding farewell to all that was familiar, all that she loved. Then she lifted her head bravely and walked out, dropping the latch behind her.

The Pascoes' schooner joined the other wagons at the edge of town, forming a group much larger than Nathalie had expected. The racket of the outfit filled her ears. Men yelled at mules and oxen. Children shouted. Cows bawled. And dogs barked. The party reminded her of excited geese. And Erman stood at the forefront, flashing a guide-book to show that he knew more than anybody about the westward trek. He spotted Nathalie and waved cheerfully.

Nathalie wondered if she were the only nervous one, the only one who felt herself cut loose from her anchor, facing dangers the like of which she had never known. Nor did her fears center on Indians or raging rivers or deserts. No, her qualms went deeper to a foe unknown, a threat to the spirit. Hers were intangible fears.

A horn sounded above the clatter. "It's time to line up," the captain shouted. "We are losin' valuable time. Erman Whitt will make the report."

Nathalie heard the reading in snatches, giving the information but half her attention. The train would be called the Winging West, or WW, outfit. A committee of six men would appoint guards, see to the livestock, and check supplies for the duration of the trip. There would be no drinking. The train would start at six o'clock each morning and cover at least ten miles a day.

"Other details can be worked out as we go along," finished Erman.

"Any more business?" asked Thaddeus.

"Yup," spoke a rangy, red-haired man. "Any single woman not akin to a traveling family should be left behind. She'll be a problem."

Tongues wagged.

Yes.

No.

Yes.

No.

Stage whispers: "He has a jealous wife, they say." "He's afeared he'll be called upon to share his supplies." "He left his own daughter behind, and he doesn't want to be reminded."

Erman beat on a tin pan with a spoon to gain attention. "Only one person falls in that category. I am sponsoring her. And she will be allowed to go, or I refuse to be your guide."

Propped against a wagon, a pudgy, bewhiskered man nudged his neighbor. "Y'hear that? He's *sponsoring* her. Came east on a wife hunt or my name ain't Jake. And to think a woman is duped by them big talkin', proud walkin' rotters!"

"You think he's that kind, eh?"

"So's I hear."

Thaddeus spoke up. "We don't want to split the train over such a small matter," he said.

The subject was dropped, but the conflict drove all peace from the unwanted traveler. At the center of the contention, she recoiled from her position.

"Any other questions?"

"What about the preacher man?" asked someone. "He don't have no money an' no vittles."

"Parsons go free," replied Thaddeus, "and live from canvas to canvas. Brother Danby might be needed for a sickness, a marryin', or a buryin'."

"Or to keep away bad spirits," prompted one.

Standing at the edge of the crowd, a sad-eyed man, skeletal from his many fasts for lost souls, jerked his head up.

"Let's vote," suggested someone.

"Aw'right. Ever'body in favor of keeping on Brother Danby 'Aye' for him," called Thaddeus.

Aye.

Aye.

Aye.

The ayes won.

Checking wagons and occupants, the six appointed committeemen made the rounds, compiling a list of names. Then they were off, and Nathalie realized that it was now too late to change her mind about going west.

She found her corner in the Pascoe wagon and sat, emotions strung tightly. Some of the children still slept, leaving her to wonder how large her "family" might be. But when the oxen had settled to a steady pace of plodding, Albert's wife moved to Nathalie's side.

"I am Maggie Pascoe," she offered. "And I'm right gladsome to have you along. Six children are a burden for one woman. The two boys are driving with Albert, but the four girls are sleeping. They are all under twelve, the lads being the eldest. Their names are Calvin and Amil. The twins, Rachel and Leah, are eight, May is five, and baby Nan is nigh on to nine months. I expect she will be starting to walk and talk good by the time we homestead in the West. And they tell me that you are a teacher?"

"I've never taught, but I could. I schooled to grade eleven and got a certificate."

"Albert said your name is Nathalie. That's a pretty name, real musical and not so plain."

"I was named for my father, Nathan Lee Thommason."

"I like fanciful names. And I don't know why anyone wouldn't welcome a pretty thing like you along."

"They are afraid that I will be a . . . a distraction."

"To whom? I don't know as anyone on the train is sweetheart looking. Oh, the Claremores have a sixteen year old, but he's too young for that. And there's the preacher, Brother Danby, but he hasn't a roving eye. He's old, anyhow. His only thoughts are taking the gospel to some new settlement."

"I want to be a blessing, not a burden, Mrs. Pascoe. I want to earn my way."

Maggie waved her hand. "Why, I'm not a whit worried. And please call me Maggie. All of us wives are glad to have another woman along so's we can talk about marigolds and dishes and pretty material. Men don't think women thoughts."

Nathalie's tension seeped away. She liked Maggie; Maggie was unpretentious. To work for her would be a pleasure.

As the children awoke, Nathalie made friends with each of them. They were all lovely children, polite and well behaved. But the baby, a golden-haired angel of happy coos and dimples, entrenched herself in Nathalie's heart, as well as her arms, with amazing alacrity, erasing the remaining traces of dubiety about the trip west.

That first day, the caravan wormed its way down hollows, across shallow streams, and through trees. Maggie had baked a gargantuan supply of salt-rising bread, and this they ate with molasses. And when they camped for the night, the captain proclaimed that they'd made excellent time with no trouble. A good omen, he lauded while Erman's expression published the fact he'd parked the success on the doorstep of his own ego.

Nathalie, glad to stretch her limbs, went to work gathering firewood for the evening meal's preparation. Unaccustomed to idle hands, she exacted no prompting. Pay her way, she would. Seeing the wagons standing white in the evening sun made her heart swell with pride. WW outfit was her outfit, and they were doing well.

The journey, she thought, was going better than she could have hoped. Maggie, a child bride and yet in her twenties, was warm and companionable. If the women of the train were jealous of a single girl, Nathalie would show them she was no challenge to their happiness. She wouldn't so much as look in the direction of their husbands! There wasn't a man in the bunch that she would want anyway.

Arms laden with kindling, she felt something touch her shoulder. In her surprise, she jumped and dropped a stick of wood.

"I'm sorry to startle you, Miss." Erman Whitt stood behind her. "I'll do that for you. I would be pleased to."

"Thanks, but I will do it myself. I need to earn my keep." She turned to walk away.

"Don't lay your mind on those who object to your going west with us." He smiled a smile that brought the blood climbing to Nathalie's cheeks. "They don't know, as I do, that something good awaits you at journey's end— or perhaps before the journey ends. We are fortunate that we have a parson in our midst. If anyone gives you a bother, you are to let me know. Is that understood?"

Nothing was understood, really. What did Mr. Whitt know that the others did not?

And what part did the parson play in it?

Nathalie slowly nodded, then broke and ran toward camp.

Chapter Five

Discouragement

The ecstasy of the trip did not last long. Like milk that gradually sours, Nathalie's days lost their sweetness with a ritual of dirt, weariness, eye-smarting camp smoke, and the cramp of limbs from long hours of sitting. Would she ever be rid of the grainy feel of sand in her shoes? Days merged insensibly into other days, each crammed with its cargo of duties, doubts, and demands.

Night brought more fatigue than the night before, exhaustion heaped upon exhaustion. In her disheartened state, Nathalie would have welcomed a train going back to Medford Mill. She'd be the first to sign on, begging to live with the family who leased her home place, to be their indentured servant! What did the West hold for her, if indeed they ever did arrive? Mr. Whitt hinted that something wondrous awaited. But what?

Maggie, by contrast, was designed for the trail. Assured. Unafraid. If the thought of steep mountains, big rivers, and trying travel depressed her, she did not voice her displeasure. But Nathalie was too soft for these rigors. She harbored a miserable disquiet that would not subside for all her prayers and self-persuasion.

Was the problem miles? Or distance? The empty expanse that defied the slow turn of the wagon wheels and the lumbering steps of the oxen? Hour by hour, the infinity of the journey loomed ahead with no hope of shortening, hills and clouds and a horizon beyond reach.

"It seems so far," she said to Maggie, discouragement shrouding her words.

"Far, it is," responded Maggie. "We all knew that it would take months to get to our destination. I don't think about the distance. I think one day at a time. I have a good wagon, a good man, and a fine brood of youngsters. We are headed for our promised land. My blessings keep me thankful."

"I think I need an attitude adjustment," sighed Nathalie.

"What you need, dear," said Maggie, "is a good man. That would make all the difference in the world."

"Good men are not plentiful."

"As Mama would say, 'Nothing truer was e'er spoken.'"

"Better no man than an unprincipled one."

"I couldn't vouch for his principles, but you have a man's glad eye right here in our company."

"Who?" The question shot out.

"The man with the map."

"Mr. Whitt?"

"Yes. He keeps a watch on you."

"He feels a responsibility for me, that's all."

"Perhaps so."

"Anyhow, he is much older than myself."

Maggie shrugged. "I dare say he isn't a day past thirty. And sometimes older is advantage."

"He is not the man for me." Nathalie was amazed by the strength of her resistance to Erman Whitt, a resistance so resolute that she seemed to feel herself retreat to gather forces to oppose the man.

That very evening when the wagons had tightened into their circle and the women disembarked, Nathalie looked around. Surely enough, she caught Erman's eyes fixed upon her. He looked away, but twice more during the meal, she found herself pinioned with his open stare. Maggie was right; he was "keeping watch" on her. She wrestled down a spasm of annoyance.

Then her petty annoyance annoyed her. His attention was merely guardianship, while she relegated it to something more. For shame! After all, he had promised the captain that he would take the responsibility for her safety. She chopped the concern from her mind.

With baby Nan cradled in her arms, she strolled toward the Pascoes' wagon. Maggie and Albert had gone for a walk to enjoy the sunset's vivid colors. She treasured the moments with the baby; nothing was like a baby's laughter to drive away desolation.

Someone touched her elbow. "May I speak with you, please? In private?" Erman stepped beside her.

"I . . . I promised Maggie that I would care for her baby while she and Mr. Pascoe went for a walk."

"You can bring the baby along." Holding her arm, he propelled her from the group. What could he want? Had she done something amiss? Disobeyed a rule, perhaps?

"There has been much grumbling about your coming on this trip," he said when out of earshot of the camp.

"Thaddeus, our captain, is especially unhappy. We are facing a dangerous and strenuous part of our journey—"

"I can't go back now," Nathalie said dryly.

"Nor do I want you to go back. What I want is to marry you so that I may care for you wholly. You did bring your wedding dress, didn't you?"

"I brought my mother's wedding gown, but the Pascoes will—"

"The Pascoes have their own problems. With eight of them, they will be fortunate if their supplies stretch to trip's end. And they will feel obligated to divide, no matter how slender their store. If you get sick or take desert fever, they will be obliged to nurse you. You are *my* responsibility."

Nathalie was silent, avoiding Erman's eyes, the best technique she had found to discourage unwanted encounters.

"I want to care for you. I am no poor man, Miss Thommason. I can provide well for a wife, and I will do my best to see that you are comfortable."

Nathalie, her emotions seesawing, felt a small wave of gratitude. Mr. Whitt was making a generous offer. Yet gratitude was no foundation for a marriage. Did she expect too much? Love and shared interests, a companionship seasoned with laughter and deepened by trust? Someone on whom she could pin her faith and hope . . . and dreams?

Certainly such an arrangement as Mr. Whitt suggested here in no man's land would be a great convenience. But married to Mr. Whitt . . . for all her life?

From where she stood, Nathalie could see the sun sliding behind the westward hills, leaving high in the sky the blaze of its going. She drew a long breath and released it wearily. So much ahead! Her path into the vistas of the unknown might lead to anywhere. But if she married Erman—

Even as she thought of it, the wide vistas seemed to narrow and darken. The light dimmed. She wanted . . . she didn't know what she wanted, she admitted helplessly to herself. But something more than Erman Whitt. Something more than "comfortable" or "convenient."

Erman observed her with brooding, unhappy eyes. At last he broke the silence. "Have you someone else in mind?"

"No one in particular," she stammered, pulling Nan more closely to her breast. "Just a—"

"A what?" His voice sharpened.

"Just a dream," she replied, her face burning.

"In a few days you will see that a caravan is no place for a dreamer," he warned, traces of asperity in his tone. "Then you will be glad to give me your hand. You will see." He spun on his heel and stalked away.

I've made him angry, Nathalie thought, going over Erman's impromptu proposal. *Perhaps I should have taken him up on his offer.*

Yet he had made no mention of love. Did he love her? No man would want a loveless union, would he? Why, then, had he asked her to marry him? She was sure that she did not love him.

Because she was troubled, Nathalie turned instinctively to the Pascoes' wagon and climbed in, closing the flap behind her. The time had come to sort out her confusion.

She tried to be objective, to set her own idealism aside.

Erman Whitt must be a very lonely man. All of the other men, with the exception of the old preacher, had wives. Loneliness led men to do strange things, things like impulsively proposing to the only single woman for miles around. Sympathy for Erman welled up in Nathalie's heart, and she understood the events of the day, lessening her resentment. If she could nurture these thoughts, giving them harborage, the ill will toward Erman Whitt would soon disappear.

For a long while, she sat reviewing Erman's overture, trying to adjust her dreams to fit his scheme. Presently, she heard voices outside.

"I should think that you are taking the Scriptures seriously about a man not dwelling alone, Mr. Whitt," Preacher Danby spoke.

"Yes," Erman agreed, "but you must concur with me, Parson. The girl has no business traveling alone. I have the means wherewith to care for her. I will treat her well. A man who won't provide for his wife is worse than an infidel. Isn't that what your Bible says?"

"It does. And that, sir, is why I am single yet. I've nought to offer a lady. A poor horse and a mug of meal won't go far in providing, though I don't doubt the good Lord to provide for myself."

"I want to be wed right away, Brother Danby. Miss Thommason has brought her wedding dress, you have a Bible, and we need nothing more."

"I'm sorry, Mr. Whitt, but I cannot feel right about performing your ceremony. Marriage is a sacrament blessed in the sight of God. I can only be an accomplice to what God sanctions. His Book says—"

The sound of the voices melted away. Nathalie strained

to hear more, but the conversation was lost to the bark of dogs.

So Brother Danby wouldn't pronounce them man and wife. He was an eccentric man, according to Maggie. Obviously, he didn't consider weddings within his jurisdiction since he wasn't married himself.

I see no reason not to marry Mr. Whitt, Nathalie chided herself, *except for my childish romantic notions. The practical thing to do is accept his offer and unburden the Pascoes. Yes, I will marry him. . . .*

At the instant of her decision, Nathalie shivered with a cold chill, a chill that roiled from the inside out, bringing a clutch of anxiety to her heart. In the distance, a wolf howled, long and low.

No, I won't marry him! Peace returned.

But why?

If only she could talk to Papa!

Chapter Six

Kidnapped

During the night, the rain came, a sudden squall, characteristic of the caprock. The sod was spongy underfoot, the atmosphere hushed.

"We are in Indian territory." Erman went from wagon to wagon, issuing his warning. "Stay close and watch the children."

Nathalie had caught a bucket of rainwater to wash her hair. She had practiced this back home, finding that the soft and fresh offering of the sky left her tresses soft and shiny.

In counting the inconveniences of the trip, Nathalie supposed they hadn't been too bad, all in all. Oh, some of the more finicky women had grumbled about cooking food over buffalo chips, the waste of the plain's shaggy animals, but when wood became scarce, they bowed to the inevitable.

"If there's nothing else to it, there's nothing else to it," Maggie proffered logically. "What the Lord wills, He wills.

We must get to our land at whatever price. We will pick up chips if need be." Nathalie gloried in her spunk.

Now Nathalie sat in the sun so that her long hair might dry. The looseness of her tresses, free from the tight braid, felt good. She removed the last of the tangles with her comb.

The danger of Indians did not cross her mind. She knew nothing of the young brave slipping along just under the crest of a ridge, moving as a wolf might travel, where he would not be silhouetted against the sky and ye⁺ where his eyes could pan the prairie. He was dressed to fade into the scenery, his breechclout made of deerskin. He carried only a light bow and quiver with a coil of rope around his waist.

He had spotted the caravan, remaining downwind from the wagons so that the animals would not catch his scent. Dropping to his knees, he began to crawl toward Nathalie. Inch by inch he moved forward, watching.

Before Nathalie had time to turn, the Indian had her locked in his arms and was dragging her from the camp. A wild sickness burst in her, and she cried out.

The likelihood of her fate came, quickly and sharply, to torture her mind. She would die. Her captor uttered a loud guttural noise and from a distance other Indians came running. There must have been a dozen of them, she reckoned in her panic, with bare torsos and shells hanging from their ears. Prayers and tears mingled.

Then the shot of a rifle cracked in the air. "Stop!"

The young Indian froze, and Nathalie saw Erman galloping up on his black horse, his gun aimed at the bronze kidnapper. An older Indian, with a hawklike nose and beady black eyes, rushed up, gesturing wildly. He yelled to the others, waving them back.

No kindness resided in the face of the old and scarred warrior. None there and none anywhere, and Nathalie thought she would faint with fright. The ancient Indian made shapes with his hands and arms, his mouth babbling unintelligible words, his eyes mean under the feathered hair. "Brave," he pointed toward the man who held Nathalie, "need squaw. Good squaw."

"No!" thundered Erman. He brought the rifle to bear again, aimed at a sentinel plant in the distance and sliced the bloom from its stem. The Indians, who had moved in closer, hunted one another's eyes, then turned them back to Erman.

"Give her back!" ordered Erman.

The Indian tightened his grip about Nathalie. He shook his head. "Squaw," he said.

"Please, Mr. Whitt," Nathalie's voice quavered, "save me."

"Give her back!" Erman demanded again. "My squaw!" He pounded his chest for emphasis.

The old-timer stepped to the forefront. "White man squaw," he said to the brave who held her.

"No!"

"Yes!"

"Trade," said the senior.

Mr. Whitt, don't let them have your gun! pleaded Nathalie's thoughts. *They will kill both of us.*

"Gun?" Erman held up his weapon.

"No!" The chief pointed, gesturing that he was content with his bow and arrows. "Horse!"

Erman dismounted and started to remove the saddle.

"No!" demanded the old man. "Saddle mine."

Erman left the saddle and took Nathalie from the arms of the young brave, who released her with obvious reluctance. The Indian ran his hand through her hair as he parted with her. "Me want squaw," he said again. "Pretty."

"Me want squaw," returned Erman.

"I can walk," Nathalie murmured, her voice a shaky whisper. "Please set me down."

"I will take no chances of losing you again," Erman said. "And I am sorry about the lie I told."

"The lie?"

"I said that you were my squaw. It was wishful thinking."

"And I am sorry that you lost your horse."

"Ah, Miss Thommason, to me you are worth more than a thousand horses."

Now she owed her life to Erman Whitt. But did that mean she owed him her heart, too?

Chapter Seven

Tragedy Strikes

Unload, load, unload . . . keep the wheels rolling. . . .

The days grew longer—and hotter. The washing and wringing and rinsing and cooking left Nathalie near the limit of her strength at night. Baby Nan became her sole joy.

The bonding of Nathalie's heart to Maggie's baby was so complete that she could hardly bear to let the child out of her sight. She fed her, bathed her, and sang to her. Could a child of her own be dearer?

"You are spoiling Nan," Maggie laughed. "How will I manage with her when you are gone?"

"Perhaps I will just go on living with you forever."

Maggie laughed. "That would be a great blessing, but I cannot hope for such a miracle. You will have your own home and your own family."

Thus, when the baby fell ill, becoming feverish and fretful, she cried for Nathalie and Nathalie attended her faithfully. Nothing stayed with the child's stomach.

"They call it the summer runoffs," Maggie explained.

"Likely she is teething. My mama had nine in her bunch, and they all had it."

"How long does it last?"

"Until the tooth breaks through."

"She will be well then?" Nathalie's brows formed a worried frown.

"She will be fine."

But Nan did not improve; each day she grew weaker. She slept for long hours, her body burning against Nathalie's shoulder.

An older woman was called to have a look at the child. "She has the flux," she said. "At this rate, she will not live more than a few hours. She is shedding the lining of her intestines."

"What can we do for her?" Pleading and prayer haunted Nathalie's voice.

"Boiled down blackberry juice cures the runs, but berry season is spent."

Nathalie watched as hope and despair wrestled in the eyes of Maggie, a brave and deserving mother. Maggie's face didn't cry; only the hazel eyes cried, leaving the sheen of tears on her cheeks. What would it be like to give up a part of oneself?

"Can we do nothing but sit and wait?" Albert asked helplessly, revealing hard patience.

"There's nary a thing anybody can do," the older woman said. "The decision rests with God now. The babe is far gone."

Nathalie stroked Nan's hand. "I can't let her go," she said to no one in particular. "She is such a lovely baby just beginning her life, and I love her so!" Tears dripped onto the infant's gown.

For what seemed an eternity, no one spoke. Then Albert's far-off voice picked up: "Our children were our reason for going west, so that they could have a better life in a new land."

"Death could have caught you as well where you came from," said the attending woman with practical bluntness. "Babies don't come with a written guarantee that they'll abide. I had two of my own take to the earth back in Arkansas."

When Nan lapsed into an unresponsive state, Nathalie passed her to Maggie. It was only right that a mother have the last moments with her dying infant. "I guess God needs another angel up in heaven," Maggie conceded. "She's going, Albert. Get the preacher."

Nathalie washed the small body, laid it out, and wrapped it in its winding sheet, numb with grief and shock. First Papa was taken from her and then Nan. How could her spirit bear more? A cry started deep inside and wrenched up, breaking out. She put her hands to her face.

The men dug a grave, and they had a simple funeral. "In my Father's house are many mansions," read Brother Danby. Nathalie listened, tired and empty, experiencing no comfort from the words. Her shoulders hunched to a choked sob.

"We will be rolling on soon," Thaddeus was saying. "We can't let winter catch us on the trail."

"Not yet, please!" Maggie implored, her face anguished past the bearing to behold. "I can't leave my baby! Can't you see? I can't go away and leave her!"

The man who placed his hand on Maggie's shoulder was Erman. "I can always find the grave for you, Mrs. Pascoe, anytime," he comforted. His kindness touched

Nathalie. "I know this trail well. And I will fix the grave where no Indian eye can spot it."

Then he came to Nathalie's side and put his arm about her. "I'm sorry," he said. "I know that you were attached to the baby. But someday you will have your own, and your heart will not ache with such vacancy. Please believe me."

Part of her wanted to pull away from him, and another part longed to lay her head upon his shoulder and weep out her heartbreak. She yielded to the part that shut him out, falling into a silence that excluded him completely.

Chapter Eight

Message in the Quilt Box

Nathalie couldn't sleep. She sat on her mattress, arms clutched around her body in an effort to diminish her inner pain. The death of her own father had not brought more despondency than Nan's death. She supposed that was because her emotions were more fragile now.

Erman Whitt tried to befriend her. He offered support. She recoiled. After his expression of sympathy, why could she not erase her juvenile resistance and accept his affection? Why did her mind—her heart—keep thwarting him? Why the distaste? The man had a fine profile, a good forehead, a strong jaw. What more was she seeking in a man anyhow? Many women would jump at the chance she spurned.

Near daylight, she fell into a troubled sleep. In her dreams, she was holding Nan and running from Erman Whitt. She awoke at once and lay trembling, a dread goring her. The rest of the trip would be long and lonely, unless—she sat up abruptly, prodded by an unbidden thought—unless she married Erman soon. And why shouldn't she? She had no cause for compunction, she told herself. The whole wagon train would probably be joyous (except the parson).

Maggie, who had tasted a child's birth and death in so brief a span, had not stirred. Quietly, Nathalie opened her trunk, rummaging for her father's Bible. *Oh, Papa, if only you were here to advise me!* Papa had wonderful judgment, an intuitive wisdom about people; he would know if Erman Whitt was truly a worthy man.

The corner of a page, a page she hadn't noticed when she packed the Book, caught her attention. In the gray light, she saw that it was a letter. Dressing at once and quickly lacing her high-topped shoes, she slid beneath the flap of the canvas, clutching the Bible.

Streaked light promised dawn, but the camp had not stirred. The travelers would rouse any time, and Thaddeus would be in a dither to break camp and move. An hour, at most, would be hers for prayer and devotion. However, an hour would be better than nothing.

Picking her way through the chokeberry bushes to the stream beyond, Nathalie sat on a fallen log. Her mind swung to Erman, kind, good Erman. She would discipline herself to like him. The Bible said one should set one's affections. That meant one's affections were his own to control. She would staunch the rebellious part of her heart! Now or later, she must conquer the foolish schoolgirl yearning for a storybook romance. That was called infatuation. Dreamers were asleep to the waking world. The slaying of that fantasy might as well be accomplished today. Heart, I will marry Erman

Whitt! She felt a slow, creeping tide of comfort.

Kind, good Erman . . .

Sympathetic, sweet Erman . . .

Gentle, nice Erman . . .

After the soul-searching—or was it a soul-scouring?—she removed the note sheet from the Bible to examine it. Her father's handwriting filled the page, infusing her with excitement. The letter was addressed to her.

My dear daughter,

You are a lovely girl and will soon be a lovely woman. I pray that I have guided you aright so that you will be able to make the proper decisions, especially in the matters of matrimony.

Listen to your heart, Nathalie. When you have found the right man, your heart will tell you. All doubts will go and you will know. Take care, and be honest with yourself. That certain one will probably not be the first to ask your hand in marriage. Do not act in haste. Never settle for less than your heart demands. Marriage is too important for you to accept second best.

My wishes for you are quite specific and may seem somewhat constricting. But if you would pursue the ultimate happiness, you must obey my mandates scrupulously. First, be certain that God and His servant, the preacher, are in agreement with the marriage. Sometimes God shows His ministers knowledge that is withheld from others.

Second, let widow marry widower. Take to yourself a man who has not given his body or soul to another woman. You are deserving of such a man.

Third, let your children be the fruit of your own body unless you take an orphan who is an orphan indeed with no living relative to spring up and cause you grief.

Next, marry a man not so far removed from your own age, neither too young nor too old for the inter-action of mind and spirit.

And, above all, select a man who loves God and country, who is in accord with your own upbringing and godly principles.

Let your heart regard neither wealth nor poverty in your decision.

If all of this you observe, you shall have a bit of heaven on earth, for true love comes without warning if the heart is truly ready.

My prayers are for you and with you.

Love,

Papa

Chapter Nine

Followed

Shaken by the letter—as if her father had seen ahead and read her thoughts—Nathalie paced the riverbank, both frightened and irritated. Just when she had made up her mind to marry Erman Whitt . . .

When had her father written the letter? How long had it been in the Bible? Did he have a premonition that he would be leaving her and that she would need guidelines? Papa's message said that she should listen to her heart. Indeed, she had almost succeeded in hushing the voice of her heart in deference to logic. Was she willing to be honest with herself?

Honesty reminded her that Erman had never spoken of love. Didn't that precede asking for one's hand in marriage? What had impelled Erman's proposal? Had someone suggested that she needed his oversight? No woman wanted a marriage based upon pity or duty. Better no marriage at all than a dutiful one.

In the mental parley, Nathalie took no notice of her

steps. Abruptly, as her foot turned on a loose rock, she lost her balance. Her hand released the letter as she plunged into the rushing river. The water closed over her head, filling her nostrils as her mouth opened wide for a scream. She choked, drew water into her lungs, then flailed her way to the surface, gasping. With but one short gulp of life-giving air, she went down again. She would surely drown.

There would be no one to mourn her passing. She would join Nan, and the caravan would move on. Somewhere in the unknown, she would meet her father and tell him that she had tried to follow his last instruction, his charge that she go west. She had died in the trying.

Nathalie's struggling ceased. She gave herself to the current.

Then from above came a hand. The hand caught her clothing, hauling her up, up. Arms lifted her, strong arms. They bore her to the surface and placed her on the bank. Hot as the day was, she began to shake not only because of her wet clothes but due to shock. She tried to sit up, water dripping from her plastered hair, down her back, and off her dress, a puddle forming around her. Her breathing labored in her chest, and she fell back.

"Miss Thommason! What happened?" Erman hovered over her with concern, his face drained of color.

"I . . . I fell into the river." Nathalie attempted to control her breathing, to steady her voice. She tugged at her water-soaked skirt in an effort to cover her calves, plainly visible above her shoes.

"You should never leave the camp without telling someone where you are going," scolded Erman. "Had I not come along just in time, you would have drowned."

Nathalie pushed the wet hair from her face. "I wanted to be . . . alone."

"Not a smart idea, my dear. Isolation on the trail is dangerous business."

"Did you follow me?"

"Mrs. Pascoe sent me to look for you. She was quite worried."

"Thank you . . . for saving my life."

"My pleasure. And I cannot let anything happen to my future wife, you see." He smiled at her. "And when may I give you that title? Each day convinces me more that you need my protection."

"I'm . . . I'm not sure that I love you."

He chuckled. "I will give you such a good life that you shall. Love in marriage is a secondary element. Love comes in its own good time."

Yes, even Papa agreed with that. He said true love comes without warning if the heart is ready.

"I don't think I'm . . . ready." The prospect of a loveless marriage, however suitable it may be, rankled Nathalie. "I don't want to marry . . . anybody . . . until I am at least twenty. Papa said that nineteen could change, be something else, by the time I am twenty."

"And when will you be twenty?"

"In . . . three weeks."

"You don't have long to do your changing, do you?" he teased. "And I'm sure I will like the changes, whatever they may be. Well, I can wait."

I've said the wrong thing, Nathalie realized too late. *I didn't mean I would marry him when I turned twenty.*

Erman set her on her feet and kissed her hand. "Are you all right?"

Nathalie snatched her hand away. "Yes, but I want to go back to the wagon."

"We will visit awhile first. At least until you dry. You look rather fetching with your clothes stuck to you like that."

Nathalie felt a flush flood her throat and face. "I . . . I don't want to visit."

"Tell me, Miss Thommason," he pressed. "Why are you afraid of me?"

"Afraid? Of you?"

"You look like a frightened fawn who has heard the roar of a tiger."

"I . . . I don't feel like a fawn."

"You know, you shouldn't be frightened of me, for I am very fond of you. And the more I see of you, the fonder I grow."

Nathalie drew back. "Your devotion is of no interest to me."

"That rather surprises me, I must say."

"I'm sorry if I have misled you."

"You haven't misled me. You have misled yourself. You are not following your heart. I know a great deal about you. You like me, but you are too stubborn to admit it."

"We hardly know each other."

"We will remedy that."

"Goodbye," she said, alarmed at the path the dialogue had taken. Turning, she stumbled toward camp with Erman following closely.

The camp buzzed with morning activity, the women readying breakfast, the men preparing to leave. Nathalie

54

looked for Maggie but did not see her.

Erman joined the men, and Nathalie had almost reached the wagon when she remembered the letter. *Papa's letter! I must have it.* Frantically she retraced her steps and found it, purposing to cloister it in the Bible again.

In the wagon, she heard Maggie's even breathing. The bereaved mother had passed a grieving night, Nathalie reasoned, and she had overslept. Nathalie moved noiselessly so as not to disturb the sleeper. She had almost finished redressing when Maggie opened her eyes.

"I'm sorry that I didn't awake in time to help with breakfast, Nathalie. I have a ghastly headache."

Erman said that Maggie sent him to look for me, puzzled Nathalie. *Something doesn't ring true.*

"You haven't been up at all this morning, Maggie?"

"No, but I will get up now."

"Please don't. I will bring your mush. Let me care for you until you are stronger."

Maggie sighed. "You are kind, Nathalie. I know that your heart is hurting for Nan, too."

"I went out early this morning to think and pray."

"I didn't even hear you leave."

"And you didn't send anyone looking for me?"

"No. Why should I? I would not have sent Albert for you unless you were in danger of being left. You are entitled to some privacy. Why do you ask?"

"Erman Whitt came looking for me."

"Surely you are aware, Nathalie, that the man follows you everywhere you go."

Chapter Ten

Erman's Plan

Thinking of his brief encounter with Nathalie now, anger stirred in Erman and found expression. He delivered a violent kick to the wheel of his wagon, then stumped blindly around the conveyance, words he would like to say to her echoing over and again in his mind. He had hoped that Nathalie might fling her arms about his neck or crumple against him in loving gratitude when he fished her from the river. In fact, working to this end, he had waited until she was thoroughly terrified before he leaped to her rescue. He could have prevented her falling into the water in the first place, as close as he lurked.

He began refining his words, rephrasing them, sharpening them, inventing more persuasive proposals to bestow upon her ears. He had no doubt that he would win. The carapace that shielded the real Erman Whitt had been adequate for a long time, the sham, the impressive front.

As he thought on his next move, his deliberation vacillated from wheedling to rage. He even pictured himself shaking her like a rag doll, shouting, "Can't you see your idiocy? I can take care of you! I can protect you! Will you see?"

He stopped in shock, dazed at the vividness of his imagined assault upon her. None of his previous endeavors had rendered him so volatile. Why was he angry? This would never do. Nathalie deserved censure, certainly, for her irresponsible behavior, for her prattle about love. But why couldn't he chide her without allowing himself to lose his aplomb?

Did he resent her self-sufficiency? Yes, he concluded, he did. But still, what if she lacked those qualities? Would he be as intrigued by her? No. At first sight of her, he had wanted her for a wife. Her dark blue eyes had enchained his attention at once; fierce independence shone from them. His alert and practiced eye approved of her well-molded figure in its simple dress of russet brown.

The resentment he experienced was clearly a part of his love for her. That she could put in peril that spirit, that beauty that he wanted for his own by carelessly falling into the river brought the outrage he felt. He could not lose her now!

Thaddeus was making the rounds, examining the wagons. "We will be coming to the fort afore long, won't we, Erman?" he asked.

"In a couple of weeks, I expect."

"The women are gettin' fidgety. They have been weaned from civilization too long. Women! If we didn't have to bother with them, we'd make much better time."

"And have grub unfit to eat. No caravan is complete without women."

"Have it your way, Erman."

"How long will we be staying at the fort?" Erman queried.

"No longer than need be. A day and a half. Two days at the most. We don't want to waste no time."

"The women won't like that. We should plan a week or two to give them some city life."

"No, Erman. The women will get town spoiled and won't want to get back in the wagons and go on. After seeing real buildings, they'll rue going back to mush and sand and jackrabbit stew."

"But I have my reasons for wanting the extra time, Thaddeus."

"No reason is good enough to dally that long."

"Then I'll dally and you can go on by yourself. Just remember, the worst of the trail is ahead."

"What's in your craw, Whitt? You have the map and you promised to see this outfit through—"

"In three weeks, Nathalie Thommason will be twenty. She won't consent to a marriage until her birthday. It is a stupid agreement she made with her father or something. At the fort, I can get the papers and a preacher. Danby won't do the honors, and I'm sure Nathalie won't marry without paperwork."

"You'll have to get the papers and marry later, Erman."

"I don't want to marry later."

"Factly, the intelligent thing to do would be to wait until you get yourself home to wed and give the girl a proper honeymoon. Does Miss Thommason know about your many . . . assets?"

"No, and you button your lip, Thaddeus. I want to surprise my bride. When she sees what I have to offer a woman, she will be glad she married me!" Under the fringe of his mustache, the corners of Erman's mouth moved slowly upward. He stuck a playful thumb into Thaddeus's ribs.

"Ah, you're as cunning as a squirrel hiding nuts, Erman Whitt. You have a lot of pride."

"I have reason to be proud. I am a successful man."

Thirteen days later, the lead wagon sunk from sight down a long slope that led to the fort. One by one, the wheels went out of sight, then the bed, then the top. And they were there, stopping beside the settlement flanked with woods.

Erman peeled his eye for Nathalie. Young men would be here who might try to woo her. She was a graceful lady! The sooner he had her in his control, the better. Until then, he would defend his rights with whatever methods necessary. And he did have rights: without his financial investment, she would be in Medford Mill yet.

He saw her entering the general store with Maggie. She'd piled her hair on top of her head for the public appearance. Jealousy bit with sharp teeth. The loose lines of his mouth tightened.

"Ladies," he bowed, "may I buy you a soda?" He had it ordered before they could answer. "Do sit in a real chair!" He ushered them to a table with a chivalrous sweep of his hand.

"Brother Danby is holding an outdoor service this evening," Maggie spoke up. "He says he'll feel like the prophet of old crying in the wilderness without Bible stand or walls. Will we have churches in the West, Mr. Whitt?"

"There's one in our village," Erman nodded, picking

his words cautiously. "Brother Danby wouldn't fit there, but I'm sure it is a church you will enjoy, Miss Thommason. You are sure to find much in common with the women who attend. And you are welcome, too, if you settle in our area, Mrs. Pascoe."

"Albert says that we will be going on to the coast, Mr. Whitt. We will join another wagon train in Oregon."

"I think that I will go farther west, too," Nathalie broached. "The farther west, the greater the need for teachers, I would think."

"The truth is, Miss Thommason," Erman intercepted, "we are in grave need of educators in our community. I told the city council that I would be on the lookout for a teacher when I went east. I can think of at least seven youngsters near me who beg an education in the future. Our clan will be delighted to have so brilliant a teacher as yourself. And we will see that you are well paid, of course."

"Does your school provide lodging for its teachers, sir?"

"Yes. Oh, yes."

"I can hardly wait to get established somewhere! When will we be traveling again?"

"I had planned to celebrate your birthday here at the fort, Miss Thommason, but Thaddeus insists that we pick up the trail the day after tomorrow. If you would like to stay here, we will. You and I. I can have the papers fixed up for our union—"

"I prefer to go with the wagons," Nathalie said, the calm dignity of her face banishing any levity from Erman's mind.

Oh, well. He would do whatever he must to humor her.

A few more days couldn't make that much difference. Wealth always turned a woman's head. When she saw his spread . . .

Chapter Eleven

Hidden Supply

At least one establishment at the fort clung grimly to its respectability. That was the general store. The day before their departure, Maggie sent Nathalie there for sassafras root. It was good, she said, for upset stomachs. She wanted it in stock when they crossed the badlands.

It was past noon. The wagons, Thaddeus announced, would roll out early the next morning. All last-minute shopping must be expedited and loading begun.

Voices arrested Nathalie as she entered the building. A deep, clear voice cut through the din. "I say, Mr. Whitt, I do not agree with you."

"I am not asking that you agree with me, Stan. You never have, and you never will. You haven't the revelation that has been granted to the Lord's few. You do not believe in the vision of my forefathers, nor have you their spiritual insight. Had you any discernment, you would see that God has blessed me above measure. Look at me. I am only thirty years old and—"

"Spiritual wholeness cannot be gauged by earthly possessions, Mr. Whitt. If that were so, Jesus would have been a wealthy man. Paul would have been rich. John the Revelator would have been prosperous. Some of the most saintly folk I know have died paupers."

"You haven't read the book—"

"If you will excuse me, Mr. Whitt, I need to be up and about my business. My son will be getting hungry soon. Since Virgie's grandmother is ill—and she had to stay with her—I brought Jeb along with me. And fine company he is, too."

Nathalie stepped to the counter in time to see a tall, honest-faced man place his hand on the shoulder of a boy whom she guessed to be six or seven years of age. Fatherly pride rode in his cobalt eyes. "This is Daddy's buddy."

Now there is a man such as I would like to find, supplied Nathalie's subconscious mind. True. Courageous. Gentle. Lucky the woman who has such a gentleman for her husband. . . .

Erman saw her and nodded. She tried to ignore him, wishing for nothing more than to make her purchase and escape. But it was not to be.

"Miss Thommason!" he assailed. "Please come here and let me introduce you to my friend."

What should she do? To ignore him in the presence of the gentleman would appear rude. She cared not what Erman thought of her, but she wanted the gentleman to think her well-bred.

"Yes?"

"Meet Mr. Stan Oliver and his young son. I was just telling him about our matrimonial plans—"

Mr. Oliver favored her with an expression of deep concern. "I'm pleased to meet you, Miss." He extended his hand, a strong hand and work-calloused. His voice was rich and sonorous. "Greet the lady, Jeb."

Timidly the child reached for Nathalie's hand, and Nathalie was smitten by his enchanting smile. "And we both wish you much happiness, Miss."

Nathalie felt too flustered to reply, too numbed to concentrate. "I . . . I am going to be a schoolteacher," she said. What compelled her to make this remark she did not know unless she hoped it would counter whatever Erman may have told the man about a romance between them. Indeed, there was no romance.

"Only if you wish," granted Erman.

"Sir?"

"Only if you wish to be a schoolteacher. You will not have to work for a living."

"I wish," sallied Nathalie. *Keep Erman Whitt talking until I can get away,* her eyes pled with the stranger, and the stranger seemed to understand her message. His head tilted ever so slightly as he plunged into a discourse that exacted rapt attention from Erman. Nathalie made her purchase and hurried out.

In the morning, the wagons rolled on—rolled on into the roughest part of the trip, a terrain of barren desert. All signs of civilization vanished. The days at the fort seemed but a vague dream, rubbed to a blur with the demands of subsistence.

Dim-witted buffaloes glared after the caravan, hoofing up dust as they fled from the flapping canvas. There were wolves, too. Wolves traveled in packs, their eyes yellow and their wet tongues extended, looking for a stray calf or an old cow too feeble to keep up. Buzzards dipped and circled in this world devoid of humanity.

Rib bones and skulls lay around on the plains claimed by prickly pear and greasewood—and a scattering of sunflowers. Broken pieces of furniture rotted along the trail, tossed aside by previous travelers as they climbed the dusty ridges.

Thaddeus planned to complete the passage through the forty-odd miles of dry land in a week, but two of the wagons broke down, necessitating an unexpected layover. Extra days were added to round up the cattle that had stampeded in a lightning storm. Troubles begat troubles, and time became the essence.

There was an odor of desiccated earth over the wasteland, and white residue lay on everything like a film of chalk. Nothing stirred. What few plants survived drooped in exhaustion, too weary to lift their arms in a plea for succor. The caravan would redeem the lost hours or join the bleached bones about them.

Sometimes they traveled all night. The whole party longed for a patch of shade and cool water. Not an oasis was there for man or animal. Fretful children clung to their mothers' skirts. Some of the livestock mired in sinkholes, and four of the eighteen had to be abandoned. The food supply, kept in kegs and barrels, ran low. In the impatient smudge of days, the hours ached and groaned. Disagreements broke out over little things and big things and things that mattered not at all.

Brother Danby walked and prayed. Where was grass? Where was water? Would they all die on the desert?

The caravan stopped only to dole out precious water to the oxen, to eat their ration of dried meat and bread.

Faces blazoned the strain, bodies drooped, and legs lagged. The pilgrims sighed with relief when the day's blistering sun slid beneath the horizon, painting a dark fire there.

Maggie became ill. "I'm glad I brought the cradle, Nathalie," she said. "If I can make it to our new home in the West, we will be blessed with a new little Pascoe. But . . . but we are running out of food."

Erman learned of the shortage. "I have an adequate supply of staples," he told Albert. "I will take Miss Thommason and give you meal and flour in exchange for her. Convince her to become my bride and the bargain is sealed. Otherwise your family will die of hunger before we reach the green."

Albert laid Erman's treaty before Maggie. It was Nathalie or food. "That is not fair!" objected Maggie. "The man is taking advantage of our starvation!"

"Fair or no, Maggie, our children cannot survive without nourishment," he said. "Please talk to Nathalie. Implore her to help us. Erman is an intelligent man and a man of means, if the trail boss's word can be relied on. Nathalie could make a worse marriage."

Maggie did talk to Nathalie, bringing into sharp focus the intensification of that intangible coercion Erman heaped upon her. *What shall I do?* Nathalie grappled with bitter feelings that beleaguered her. *I cannot let Maggie, who is nurturing a new life, lack for provisions. O God, help me! Show me what to do! I am willing to sacrifice myself for others, but I had rather die than be locked in a union that is not of Your making.*

Then Nathalie remembered the rabbit jerky, the dried fruit, and the nuts stowed in the bottom of her quilt box.

She had forgotten about packing the food.

"Tell Mr. Whitt that we will not need his resources," Nathalie told Maggie. "God will provide for us. I have food enough for several days in my trunk."

From the supply in the box, the Pascoe family and Nathalie—along with Brother Danby—ate grandly until shade and pasture and water spread before them and their gaunt stock. They had lost no wagons and no people. And Nathalie was spared from an unwanted marriage.

Chapter Twelve

The River

The summer was gone, the foretaste of autumn in the air. Thaddeus goaded them now, putting in longer days and allowing for shorter stops. After the last challenging river, they would be in Oregon. By winter, he baited, they would be building their cabins.

"I hope that I have been worth my fare," Nathalie told Maggie when she learned that there was but one more river to ford. "I owe you so much."

"You owe us nothing, Nathalie."

"But you brought me in your wagon—"

"It was an agreement with Erman Whitt. He paid us to bring you. But even if he had given us no money, we would have been glad for your company—"

"Mr. Whitt paid you to bring me?"

"Yes."

"But he said that I would be earning my way by working for you, by helping you with the children."

"Mr. Whitt is a mystery, Nathalie. Let's not even try to

decipher him."

Then came the Snake River, an obstacle that was every dread Erman had promised. As Nathalie peered over the lip of the gorge to the frothy ribbon of water below, a whirlpool between high banks, turbulent and unruly, she dubbed it the most tormented water she had ever seen. The bottom, if there was one, was out of sight. Waterfalls, running silver, sent curtains of liquid catapulting thunderously downstream. Nor was the torrent a blockade that took the easy way. Would they ever get to the other side?

When they reached the crossing, though, it wasn't as intimidating at close range. Just as the sun swung above the hills, they started across. Oxen stepped into the rushing waters, staring at the distant shore as if to calculate their chances of survival. The current bucked against them, yet they lined out, swimming hard, their chins flattened on the surface.

To Nathalie, it seemed that the opposite bank swam to meet them. They would be across this wild, bottomless water by noon. Like weather, the actuality wasn't as bad as the forecast. One wagon made it, then two, then three.

Albert hitched six yokes to the Pascoe schooner because of its larger size. All was going well. The wagon rode safely above the ripple. Then it happened suddenly, without rhyme or reason, as they neared the far shore. The lead animal thrashed for footing, wrenching its mate along. Their weight dragged the second yoke down as the wagon slanted toward the frightening depths. The vehicle skidded, swinging this way and that, grinding over gravel. The shore moved away.

Maggie screamed, the sound lost in the noise of the

water. Then the swinging wagon caught on a submerged boulder while the current tore at it. Wedged between the rock and the wash, the wagon flipped onto its side.

Nathalie, hurled into the power and muscle of the raging fury, tried to fight the waves that lapped her face—but could not. Rising before her, the great hulk of the overturned wagon fell away and rose again, looming, towering, its bottom dark and monstrous. It was crashing down on her! Kicking, kicking, kicking . . . her muscles throbbed; her clothes were leaden. As if resenting her escape, the water clutched her.

There were voices. "The rope! Miss Thommason, catch the rope!" Someone ran along the distant shore, his arms swinging. A rope looped toward her. But her arms were heavy and her throat strangling. There was water. And the voice. And more water. And the voice.

The rope caught her about the shoulders, and she was being hauled in.

"She can't be dead—"

"She wasn't there long enough to drown."

"Nathalie!"

"Easy," Erman said, turning Nathalie on her stomach to pump the water from her lungs. She lay prone, her nose pressed against the ground, digging both hands into the earth, unaware that the ordeal was over.

"Are you okay, Nathalie?" Maggie's voice reached her.

Nathalie moaned.

Big hands pressed her rib cage. "She'll make it," Erman informed. "I can feel the life in her. Now if she had been in my wagon, Albert, this wouldn't have happened."

He turned her over. The clatter of voices around her, the host of faces merged into a jumble of sight and sound, and for a moment, she could neither focus her eyes nor attend with her ears. Her quizzical look traveled from face to face, asking why she was on the ground with people looking at her. "Papa!" she called hoarsely before remembering that her father was dead.

Her eyes filled and her face twisted, but she was all right except for the crying. Directly she sat up, assisted by Thaddeus and Erman.

"She'd best rest awhile," Maggie said, spreading a blanket on the ground as the women flocked about her.

"Everything went well," someone joined the crowd to publish. "Nothing but some plunder wet. It lacks believing, but that wagon just coasted into shore."

They had bested the Snake without a loss; the days of peril were past. "And it's home from here," a subdued sojourner reflected.

Home? Nathalie sensed the song in the blood of her fellow travelers. Within their reach was rich soil waiting for seed, tarrying for willing hands and for the happy cries of children. But her own heart gave no answering cry. Would she ever have a home?

Down went her head on her arms, and she gave way to wracking sobs, not for the emptiness of today but for the barren yesterdays and the bleak tomorrows. How dismal, how colorless, how meaningless the canvas of her life had become, crowded with forbidding, horrible shapes. She released a volley of tears that had run for days through the dark and secret places of her being. They were better out of her. Held in, they might destroy her.

"Oh, Papa!" she whispered. "Why did you tell me to go west?"

Chapter Thirteen

Erman's Manor

As the hours of their pilgrimage dwindled, the good-byes began. The wagon train was breaking up.

"I've made my decision, Maggie," Nathalie stated. "I am going on with your family. I feel . . . inside . . . that I should. My heart doesn't say 'stop' yet."

This was the moment of truth, and Maggie, not without tears, relayed Erman's unmitigated terms to Nathalie. If Albert insisted on taking Nathalie farther west, then he must repay Nathalie's portage. Every cent of it. Albert didn't have the twenty-five dollars, which meant that Nathalie would be dropped off at Erman's place in Sweet Springs and the Pascoes would go on from there.

Anxiety possessed Nathalie to the exclusion of all reason. She felt helpless and desperately afraid. Maggie, firm in spirit and tough in trials, had been her anchor. What would moor her now? To cry out her disappointment might bring relief, but that would be inexcusably inconsiderate when all the other travelers were rejoicing in their new world. She pinched back the tears.

While family after family bade one another goodbye, Nathalie waved farewell to her happiness. Forget the laughter and joy of sharing a beloved's thoughts and hopes. Forget romance. Forget dreams. Now she could never follow her heart. Inadvertently, she had sold her soul to Erman Whitt with no hope of ransom. Despondency beat upon her without mercy and without pause.

"Albert offered to earn the money and repay Erman later," Maggie was saying, "but Erman wouldn't hear to it. And Thaddeus, the trail boss, took Erman's side. Why, Albert even offered our cattle for you, Nathalie, but Erman said he has pastures full of cows at home."

Nathalie bit her lip and nodded. "Give my thanks to Mr. Pascoe for trying, Maggie."

"I wish there was something I could do for you, Nathalie. But perhaps this is for the best after all. Erman says that you will lack for nothing. That's more than even my Albert can promise."

"But you have . . . love."

"Love is a many faced creature. Mayhap you just aren't recognizing love."

No, Nathalie's heart declared, *if this is love, I can't see its face.*

The caravan slowed, and Erman came to the Pascoes' schooner. "We are almost home," he smiled at Nathalie, a smile she did not return, "and I am glad."

"I want to go farther west with Maggie's family," Nathalie said with stubborn insistence. "Maggie needs me."

"You do not understand, Nathalie, dear," Erman's

explication bore a note of disdain as if he placated a fret-ful child. The sound of her given name falling from his lips sent a sudden furious rebellion riding in her. He spoke as if she knew nothing, could not make her own choices.

"Perhaps you do not understand," she retorted.

He ignored her rejoinder. "I will give you the very best of everything. You shall have anything your heart desires. You will be glad to be my wife. That, I promise."

"I will get a job as a teacher." She lifted her chin. "I don't wish to marry."

"School has already commenced this year. It will be next year—"

"But you said you had been sent to look for a teacher."

"Everyone knew that I would marry the teacher. So you are as good as wed, you see. And I am not accus-tomed to being treated like a spoonful of medicine that must be taken!"

"I'm sorry, Mr. Whitt."

"Call me Erman!"

"Yes, Mr. Whitt."

"And surely you wouldn't accept financial assistance from a gentleman without the benefits of wedlock? That would not be proper, now would it?"

You are trapped, Nathalie Thommason, and the sooner you put away your resistance, the better. With her arguments, she merely built walls to climb over.

"Yes, Erman. I mean, no, Erman. Your offer of mar-riage is an honor, I'm sure. Thank you and good day." She didn't even attempt to camouflage her sarcasm.

"You will love me," he said flatly. "But if you never do, I will give you a reason for living."

Did romance really matter so much anyway? Nathalie combed through her heart. Erman's plea was so sane, so practical. Romance was for fairy tale princesses, not lone women stranded in Oregon. She ripped at the tiny vines of bitterness that threatened to root in her heart. Her dreams must die. Wasn't any life better than no life at all? The object was to make the most of life, whatever it dispensed. Accept what you cannot change; that's what Papa would say. *Oh, Papa, can I ever really accept Erman Whitt?*

Then they were there. It was the first of October, a time when trees wept yellow leaves. *Weep for me, maples.*

"Oh, Nathalie!" squealed Maggie. "Look! Look at your home. Isn't it grand? Almost I would trade places with you. Oh, I do wish you happiness."

Don't wish me happiness, Nathalie denounced. *I don't expect to be happy, even in such a manor. Wish me courage and strength and fortitude. I will need them all, for my marriage will be nothing more than a commonsense agreement.* Yes, she had feelings— hurts and wishes and wants—like any other girl. But she would seal them inside herself, and someday they would dry so that not even her eyes would leak.

Erman's house, in the bright sun of early afternoon, radiated newness and elegance, reminiscent of a grand lady in a new gown. The facade was three stories tall, a profusion of wood and stone. A high, narrow porch introduced a set of ornate doors. Over the doors, a shield wore the scrolled letter "W," prominent and imposing. Tall fluted columns rose to the roof, and greenery cascaded from window boxes and poured from iron urns. Obviously

Erman had not exaggerated his wealth.

"Just think! All this will be yours, Nathalie!"

"It . . . it is lovely," Nathalie grudged.

"Ooh! How many rooms do you suppose the castle has?"

"I couldn't guess, but you will come to see me when I am the mistress, won't you?" Nathalie took Maggie's hands. "And you may have any room you wish."

"You won't even remember a poor little migrant—"

"I will never forget you." Nathalie meant to give Maggie a quick hug, but instead she clung to her.

Erman came to unload her trunk and found Nathalie embracing her friend. "Come along, Nathalie," he demanded curtly. "You've had weeks to speak your piece to Mrs. Pascoe. You are mature enough to forget your mawkishness and welcome a higher strata of life."

Erman invited no one into his home for food or water; rather, he seemed to hurry them on their way. "I know that you are anxious to be on the trail," he said to Thaddeus, "and I won't delay you. I'm pleased that we made the trip with so few losses, and I bid you a successful journey henceforth."

The women came to the gate to offer their best wishes to Nathalie. Last of all, Brother Danby came. He gripped her hand, holding it longer than necessary. "Keep thy heart with all diligence," he quoted, "for out of it are the issues of life. Ponder the path of thy feet, and remove thy foot from evil."

What did the preacher mean by that? She was on the point of asking when Erman appeared to escort her to the house, hurrying her along. He had set Nathalie's mattress, chair, pillow, and box on the porch. "We will find you an unoccupied bedroom," he said. "There will be others who will be living with us. I built the house to accommodate ten families."

The wagons pulled away, severing from Nathalie everything familiar. *It is time to part with my childish notions as well,* she resolved. Today she would become an adult, with adult thoughts and actions. Why not be a good wife for Erman Whitt?

Inside the massive sitting area, Nathalie's eyes traveled from the fireplaces at each end, over the crystal chandelier to a long sideboard crowded with silver buckets and stemmed goblets. It was lovely: the dim blue of the hangings, the shining walnut and rosewood, the damask upholstery, the high, faintly tinted ceiling, the picture above the mantel of girls leaning from a balcony. What would her father think if he could see her now, soon to be the wife of a prosperous Westerner? Why had her ungrateful heart balked?

There would be servants, of course. And with other families letting rooms, she would never be lonely. Hers would be the life of a real lady. And as spouse of the landlord, she'd command a certain prominence over the tenants. The building blocks for sublimity lay at her feet. Why had a man like Erman Whitt chosen her? And after she had been rude to him!

He had saved her life thrice, and whatever dreams the child in her dredged up—of flowers and kisses and romance—she had to admire his courage. It took courage and endurance to come to an untamed land and amass a fortune. Many maidens her age would treasure such a man, such an opportunity.

Why, this would be better than a match of her own

whittling! She would dictate to that unruly heart of hers! She would teach it gratitude . . . which would lead to admiration . . . which would lead to devotion . . . which would lead to love. . . .

Chapter Fourteen

Getting Acquainted

A sprightly young woman named Hortense showed Nathalie to her quarters, a first-floor room at the rear of the house, facing the river. The dark-eyed girl, who had the butterfly prettiness of extreme youth complete with flitting movements, bright coloring, and engaging charm, fussed for an instant with the curtains, the bedding, and a rack of towels. "Welcome to Whitt House, Miss," she smiled. "We shall be great friends. Erman says that you will be one of us."

"Yes," Nathalie answered, her mind settled at last. "I have come to stay."

"That is good," Hortense affirmed again. "Here you will be cared for well. Erman will supply all of your needs."

The chamber was large and comfortable. Usurping the center was a large canopied bed. A marble washstand held a display of aromatic toiletries. A wardrobe towered against the far wall and by the window was a dressing table with a mahogany-framed triple mirror, which returned three aspects of her face, the face of Mrs. Erman Whitt.

When Hortense took her leave, Nathalie sprawled upon the great four-poster bed, feeling queenly. *Home.* This was home. At last. Here were all the symbols of secure existence: the thick, staunch walls of the house, the sturdy chimneys, a place of order with nothing near which did not accord with sobriety and propriety. *Papa, I have arrived.* The trials of the trail were fading . . . Maggie was fading . . . her silly dreams were fading. . . .

Weary in body and mind, she fell into a deep slumber, fully clad, and did not awaken until the sun rose the following morning. Then, upon rousing, her hand touched the silk of the comforter. Her bones didn't ache. There was no grit on her face. The smell of canvas and smoke and animals was missing. Had she died and gone to heaven?

"Shhh. We mustn't disturb Miss Thommason," Nathalie heard a whisper from beyond her bedroom door.

"But, Madre Hortense, I want to meet her."

"You may meet her when she has rested, Grover."

Water stood in the pitcher, clean towels and scented soap on the washstand. Nathalie refreshed herself, then stepped into the hall.

"Oh, there you are, Miss Thommason!" greeted Hortense cheerfully. "Good morning. Did you rest well?"

"Wonderfully!" laughed Nathalie. "Did I sleep for a week?"

"Almost," Hortense grinned. "But we are glad you rested. This is one of the children of Whitt House. His name is Grover. He has been impatiently waiting to meet you. He is seven."

"Hello, Grover," Nathalie said, liking the child at once.

"I'm pleased to meet you, Miss Thommason." The child took her hand in both of his, the epitome of politeness. "Welcome to Whitt House."

"Thank you, Grover."

"Erman left word for you, Miss Thommason, that he is gone for the elder to perform your wedding ceremony and that they will be back on the third day from now. In the meantime, you are to relax and prepare your wedding dress."

"I shall do that."

"This is your home. Look about as you like. The Abana room, the Shiloh room, and the Moriah rooms are all occupied. Otherwise, the run of the house is yours. There's a pianoforte in the parlor. Do you play?"

"No, but I hope to learn."

"Grace can teach you. She has enough music stored in her bones to share with the whole world! She is teaching the children. How old are you?"

"I'm twenty."

"Perfect! I am twenty-one. I came to the territory two years ago. I think the younger one's age, the more easily one can adapt to the lifestyle of the West. We live in a rather isolated area: no shops or cafes or salons are readily accessible to us. Erman gets our necessities, though, so that we feel no lack. And now and then a supply wagon comes through."

"I will be quite comfortable, I'm sure," Nathalie said. "Actually, I am not accustomed to finery."

"Oh, I wasn't either!" chirruped Hortense. "But it doesn't take long to learn, does it? And it's such fun! Your family did not object to your leaving, to your marrying Erman?"

"I have no family. My father died shortly before I left Medford Mill. My cabin was . . . repossessed."

"You were lucky that Erman came by then, weren't you?"

"Yes. Yes, I was."

"Perhaps you are fortunate not to have a family. My family objected bitterly to my coming west. They haven't forgiven me yet."

"My father wanted me to come west. That was his dying request."

A bell jangled. "Oh, there's the breakfast bell! I'll show you to the breakfast table."

She led the way to a great windowed alcove where an elaborate meal waited: hotcakes and sausages, hominy and gravy, and scones served with sweet butter and orange honey. After the seating, Hortense introduced Nathalie to the other occupants of the house, three women and seven children. The menfolk, Nathalie gathered, had already left for work.

They were a nice-looking lot, neat and orderly. The youngest of the women, at nineteen, was blessed with a new baby whom the others cared for as if it were their own. The baby reminded Nathalie of Nan, bringing a pang to her heart and a hunger to her arms. When she became well acquainted, she could cuddle the baby, too.

The oldest of the group, whom Nathalie, though never good at estimating age, guessed to be on the long side of thirty, eyed Nathalie suspiciously. Nathalie could sense the latent animosity that crackled about her like embers from a disturbed fire. The reason for it she could not conjecture, and she smiled at the woman often, trying to disarm the umbrage. Still there was trouble in the woman's eyes as though thoughts crowded behind them until even their color seemed distorted by the offense that was there. Her name was Odene. Two of the children were hers.

Nathalie offered to help with cleaning up, but Hortense said no, that she would have her chores assigned after her marriage. For the next three days, she would be treated as an honored guest. *Assigned chores?* Nathalie mused. *Mrs. Erman Whitt will call the shots in three days.*

However, Erman did not return in three days. He did not return in six. Two weeks elapsed, and in that interim Nathalie learned the household schedule. The children emptied scrap buckets, tended the refuse fires, and attended lesser details. The older ones worked at their books. However, Nathalie learned little about the families who roomed there.

Each day Odene watched her with open hostility, once seething through clenched teeth, "We don't need more people in this house! If you were smart, you would take your trunk and be gone." Anger mottled her cheeks. She seemed jealous of Nathalie, flinging the javelin of hatred at every chance, though Nathalie gave her no reason for the mistrust. *When I become the mistress of this house,* Nathalie promised herself, *Odene will change her attitude or move out.*

Nathalie marveled that she had still met none of the menfolk. Were their hours such that they arose earlier than their wives and returned late? Grover had mentioned his father a time or two but was given no opportunity to converse with Nathalie about his family. The other women stayed in their rooms when not busy.

Erman had much cattle and many horses. Hortense

cared for the livestock, and Nathalie followed her around the barn to stem boredom. Of all the boarders, Hortense was Nathalie's favorite. The two, Nathalie surmised, would become fast friends.

"Where did Mr. Whitt gain his wealth?" she asked Hortense.

"He inherited it from his father. Grandpa Whitt was childless save for Erman, and that left Erman the sole heir. Erman will have plenty to pass to all his children and grandchildren. I'm glad that you have come to be a mother."

"I am, too," Nathalie said, wondering what was keeping her future husband. When would he return for their wedding?

On the fourteenth day, Erman arrived with the elder and a pretty, soft-eyed girl whom Nathalie supposed to be the elder's daughter. Erman was in high spirits, jovial and full of small talk with the children of Whitt House. "I hope that your wedding dress is in order, Nathalie," he said, taking her hand in his.

"Indeed it is, my dear Erman." Rapture filled her, tingling her nerves. She would be married today! She, Nathalie Thommason, would become Mrs. Erman Whitt with a house of her own, the most handsome house in the West—and perhaps the richest husband.

"Ah, what a pleasure to hear your endearment," he purred. "I perceive that you like your new home?"

"Oh, I do, sir! It is lovely!"

"You seem very happy."

"I am, sir, and all because of you."

"Nonsense!" he laughed, but he looked pleased. He extended a hand toward his guests. "This is Elder Paul and Eleanor," he introduced. The elder, with somber clothes and dole face, fit the role of an ancient prince of the church, full of years and wisdom. He nodded an acknowledgment to Nathalie.

"You are ready then, Nathalie?"

"Oh, yes, sir!"

"I will summon one of the women to help you dress for the ceremony," he said.

Then he winked at Eleanor, a wink that Nathalie found very disconcerting.

Chapter Fifteen

The Exposé

"This wedding dress belonged to my mother," Nathalie explained to Hortense. "She wore it when she wed Papa."

"It is beautiful," Hortense admired, rubbing her hand over the sleeve's silky texture. "And I know that you are excited." She fastened each tiny button with a pat.

"I am. At first, I thought I didn't like Erman. But his kindness won out. He saved my life three times. And he traded a horse for me!" She laughed. "I hope he got the best of the trade!"

"Erman always wins! After today, you will truly be one of us. The children are anxious for another 'madre' as they call you."

"You are married, Hortense?"

"Yes. I've been married for two years."

"Tell me about your wedding."

"Oh, it took place right here!"

"What was your wedding dress like?"

"It was grand. Long and white with a lot of rich lace trim. Erman bought it for me."

"Erman?"

"Yes. He would have bought yours had you needed one. He is very generous."

"Tell me about your husband."

"My husband?"

"Yes—"

"Why, Erman is my husband, of course!"

"Erman? Are there two Ermans? Is everyone in the West named Erman?"

"No, there's only one, but one is enough for all of us."

"What do you mean?"

"Men of Erman's faith have many wives. They live here in the territory, since the laws of the Republic prohibit polygamy."

"You mean—" Nathalie choked. "All of you are his wives?"

"Yes, there are three of us. Odene, Grace, and I. And now he has brought Eleanor, too, and with you that will make five! You and Eleanor will have a double wedding. I can't guess which of you will have the first honeymoon, but, oh, I hope that it may be you!"

"But I don't—"

"We'll have a wonderful time together! I say, the more the merrier. All of us are happy except for Odene. She's the cook and an excellent one at that. She would like to be Erman's one and only. I suppose she thought she would be the 'exclusive' when she married him. She was his first bride. Sometimes I think she would leave if she could. But she has no resources of her own and no place to go. And then, if she went, he'd keep her children. She bitterly resents every new wife that comes here. But pay her no mind—"

"I—"

"What is the matter, Nathalie? You are shaking."

Only by adroit mastery of her eyelids, hands, the muscles of her face could Nathalie conceal the shock she had received. "I . . . it isn't right, Hortense, for a man to have more than one wife."

"Why not? Jacob in the Bible had two wives. And wise Solomon had seven hundred, although I don't think our Erman could support that many!"

"But that wasn't God's plan from the beginning."

"Why, it is a marvelous plan! We help each other and we share the workload. When one of us is sick or has a new baby, the others take her place. And Erman provides well for us. Who could ask for more in life?"

Nathalie was aghast. Anger, hurt, and outrage commingled. The whole color and shape of her day had changed. "I've never heard of such!"

"Many men like Erman live in Utah. It is God's plan for a man to have many children. David, in Psalm 127, said, 'Lo, children are an heritage of the LORD. . . . Happy is the man that hath his quiver full of them.' By being a wife to Erman, you will be a handmaid of the Lord."

She believes what she is saying, marveled Nathalie, staggered by Hortense's revelation. "But the Bible says that a man should love his wife as Christ loves the church. An earthly union, according to the apostle Paul, is a pattern of Christ and His bride. Christ has only one bride—"

"We have our own book, Nathalie. The words in it were given to our elders in a vision. It has been written since the Bible, and, therefore, it supersedes the Bible. Of course, you won't have to share all of Erman's beliefs, but he will expect you to respect them and let your children learn his doctrine."

"I don't believe I'd like to be in Erman's harem," Nathalie bit out, her moral sense offended.

"It is too late to change your mind now. You are committed, and Erman will not release you. You are to be the schoolteacher for all our children."

Nathalie's skin prickled as though a spider with icy feet crept across the nape of her neck. Hopelessness threatened to swallow her. "But he didn't tell me that he had other wives. He deceived me!"

"You'll be glad that he did, Nathalie. Trust me. After the shock wears away, you will fit into the system nicely. I felt the same way you did at first. Then I saw the sense of it all. The convenience. Now I wouldn't have it any other way."

Poor Hortense! How deluded she was. But Nathan Thommason would turn over in his grave if he knew that his daughter had joined herself to such an evil practice.

What had Papa's letter said? *All doubts will go. . . .*

Be honest with yourself. . . .

He will probably not be the first to ask for your hand. . . .

Marriage is too important to accept second best. . . .

Marry a man who has not given his body or soul to another woman. . . .

Wed a man who is in accord with your upbringing and godly principles. . . .

No, Erman Whitt was not that man.

Chapter Sixteen

Runaway Bride

The urging in Nathalie's soul became intense and compelling. She must escape this bondage or die with the trying! Now she understood; now she knew. She could not feel right about marrying Erman Whitt on the trail because he was not a worthy man. Her heart had tried to warn her.

Brother Danby tried to warn her. "Remove thy foot from evil," he had quoted. Had he known, or was his spirit troubled by a premonition? The man in the store, Stan Oliver, tried to warn her with his concerned look. What if she had married before she had learned? She shuddered, a soul quake that started at the core of her being and erupted on the surface.

The problem was *how* to escape. Her mind whirled and churned, a tornado of prayers flying about in her head. "I would like a few minutes of privacy before the ceremony, please, Hortense," she said evenly, tossing Hortense a costly smile. "Tell Erman that I will come to him when I am ready. He should allow two or three hours before expecting me. Eleanor may give her vows first, if she would like."

"You won't need me?"

"No, and please say nothing of our conversation." She gave the dark-eyed girl a hug.

Hortense stepped out, and Nathalie latched the door behind her. She had to think—coherently. She must prime her mind to the problem, marshaling at once the past, present, and future in a neat array that would spell an answer that would untangle the sordid threads of this imbroglio.

She wished—oh! how she wished—she had never come west. She longed for her spare little cottage in Medford Mill, from which she was exiled forever. If only she could sit by the fireplace with her father as he warmed his stocking feet, wiggling his toes to express comfort! But it was too late for that, and wishing accomplished nothing. This was a time for action.

The window! If she could escape through the window and flee to the river before her absence was discovered . . .

Her hands worked independently of her mind. They removed her father's Bible and her mother's doll from the quilt box, rejecting the encumbrance of quilts and clothing. Then following an inner stimulus, she slid from the opening, thanking God that hers was not a second- or third-story room. Had she been upstairs, though, she would have chanced the jump.

The valley did not provide an abundance of hiding places, but trees stood along the river. If she could get to a road, she might hail a cart. Or she might stumble upon a dwelling where a sympathetic farmer's wife would hide her. At any rate, she would prefer death by starvation or exposure to a marriage such as Erman Whitt planned for her. Death would be more honorable, and her soul would be more likely to reach heaven intact.

She hoped Erman would wait the "two or three hours" she had requested. That would give her time to distance herself from Whitt House before he discovered her truancy. Maybe beautiful Eleanor would keep him occupied.

Prayers poured from Nathalie's lips, from her heart. Fervent prayers. "Forgive me, God, for doubting my heart, for overriding what You were trying to tell me," she entreated. "I will see that it doesn't happen again. Keep me safe, and bring me to Your perfect will." She was ashamed for the many times she had silenced the deeper stream of consciousness flowing through her, squelching the truth her heart urged, not letting the awareness shape itself into thought.

While her lips prayed, her feet ran, eating up a mile, then two. She ran frantically, bent only on escape. Her legs ached; her head pounded. Then winded, she slowed her pace. To preserve her strength, she would have to walk, not run. Already, she thirsted, feeling the need for nourishment.

She traveled west, her direction evidenced by the dropping sun which had long since passed its zenith. The warmth of the pleasant afternoon would not last. There would be night and falling temperatures. A temptation to take a shortcut through the groves was foiled by the fear of becoming lost. To become lost would be to squander yet more precious time. She refused to think of what she would do if, at the end of day, she hadn't found a shelter.

Once she heard a noise behind her and froze. Was

Erman coming for her? Would he have her back and make her a participant in his delusion? *Any future but that, Lord.* But the commotion was only a small rodent scurrying through the grass.

Another hour passed, and panic tore at Nathalie's throat. She had seen no houses, no place for human habitation. Then she topped a rise, came to a knoll, and beside the road stood a wagon, hitched and ready to make a trip.

With no one in sight, Nathalie climbed into the back of the conveyance, pulled a stack of empty burlap bags over herself . . . and waited.

She hoped the wagon went fast and far.

Chapter Seventeen

Missing

Erman waited, too.

He had strictly forbidden any of his wives or their children to disclose his polygamy to Nathalie. That was his way. Capture, then reveal. And for this girl, he particularly lusted. Breaking her resistance to the system would be an amusing venture. The willing wives weren't nearly as interesting.

Erman had ordered a grand dinner with an enormous wedding cake for the celebration. The meal was ready, hosted by a grim-faced Odene. Candles glimmered, cut glass reflecting their light. Grace sat at the piano, playing soothing music.

Erman waited two hours. Three hours. Four hours. Then his patience lost its tenuous hold. He blustered his way to Nathalie's room and pounded on the door. This girl needed to be taught a thing or two; she had lingered long enough!

"Nathalie? Nathalie, darling, we are waiting."

No answer.

"Nathalie? Are you asleep?"

No answer.

He tried the knob and found the door locked, which irked him the more. What was the girl up to now? He went for the skeleton key. "I'm coming in, Nathalie, ready or not."

Erman found the room empty, the window agape. Where was Nathalie? If that little snip had abandoned him—! His anger and frustration blended into a savage emotion for which he had no name. The desire for vengeance swept to life like gray embers flaring in a sudden gust of wind. He would find her! And he would make her pay!

Through the household he went, accosting Odene first. "Where is Nathalie Thommason?" he barked.

"I neither know nor care," she retorted, her tongue tipped with malice.

"You said something to her, didn't you?" he accused. "You ran her off with your poison tongue!"

"It's a lie, Erman Whitt." Odene's eyes blazed with indignation. "I didn't even talk to the girl, though it would have pleasured me to tell her what she was getting herself into. Live and let live; that's all I ever asked of life. I've done harm to no one, except myself when I married you. And what do I get? A harpy man who sees all my faults and none of his own. Who does all the work around here? Who cooked your fancy wedding meal? You know who does it, and I get not an ounce of appreciation; and with every new woman bringing new work for me—"

Odene kept ranting, but Erman didn't stay to hear more. He should rid himself of her, he chided, but she was indispensable. She did the lion's share of the work. And her children would be fitful without her. Let her have her raving so long as she slaved for him.

Next, he confronted Grace at the piano. "Have you seen Nathalie, Grace?"

Her eyes widened, big and innocent. "Why, no, sir, I haven't. Should I try to locate her for you?" Reaching out, she touched his sleeve lightly with the tips of her fingers. "I'm so glad to see you." She swayed toward him with a wistful smile. The whole of her—vitality, will, and brain—was engaged in making herself desirable to him.

"Nathalie is not in her room. I fear she has fled."

"Why would anyone want to flee from a wonderful life with you, my love? Surely she is but playing a game of hide-and-seek—"

"I will find her, Gracie, and after our big celebration, I will come back to you." He bent to kiss her upturned face. She was his favorite.

To Hortense he went lastly. She was the youngest and most empty headed of his wives. "Hortense, Nathalie is not in her room. Do you know where she might be?"

"She was in her room but a while ago. I heard her stirring around. Have you looked on the veranda? She is a wanderer, that one. She often followed me to the barn—"

"I've looked everywhere."

"But surely she will show up soon. She was so very excited about the wedding. She could hardly wait and hoped that she might have the first honeymoon. Why, she told me about your kindness to her on the trail. How you saved her life and how you traded your horse to the Indian for her. She said that made her love you so very much and that she hoped you got the best of the trade and—"

"You didn't say anything to offend her?"

"Oh, mercy, no!" she lied. "Nor did Grover. Grover loved Nathalie. He was looking forward to Nathalie becoming his teacher. Why, Nathalie had grand plans! She wanted Grace to teach her to play the pianoforte. She said she felt so very fortunate to be chosen by you to be your bride. You don't suppose—?"

"Suppose what?"

"That something terrible happened to her? That she was kidnapped? Oh, you don't suppose she was stolen, do you, Erman?"

"Kidnapped? *Kidnapped?* By whom?"

"Oh, I don't know." Hortense wrung her hands. "Maybe the driver of the supply wagon. He came by earlier in the day."

Erman slapped his hands together. "For once, you have a thinking head, Hortense. That is a very likely possibility." In Erman's heart, a demon clamored to be heard. "And if that be so, Hortense, I will see the man hanged from a tree for stealing my woman and the yet unborn children she could give me."

"You can't be faulted for feeling thus, sir."

"I believe I can better tell what happened if I can look about her room."

They moved quickly to the room Nathalie had occupied. "See, Erman. Her luggage is yet here. And the dress she wore before she changed lays on the bed. Had it been her decision to leave, she would have taken her personal belongings. And she wouldn't have worn her wedding dress, now would she? Isn't that evidence that she was taken against her will?"

"Which way did the salesman go from here?"

"He went west. In a matter of conversation, he said he was headed home. I asked him where home was, and he said he lived southwest of Portland."

"Then he'll be obliged to take the Dove Creek Road. I will follow him! I will find him! And I will have my bride back."

"I think that hanging would be justice for the thief, sir."

"Pack my portmanteau, Hortense, and with all speed! Tell the elder and Eleanor that I will return promptly. My poor, poor Nathalie. How frightened she must be. Kidnapped!

"Well, I saved her life three times. This time, I will not only save her life, but I will save her soul as well. She hasn't read the book; she doesn't know about the vision. My poor, poor Nathalie!"

Chapter Eighteen

Surprise Passenger

When the wagon started with a jerk, striking Nathalie's head on the wooden floor, she didn't flinch. A little spring had broken inside her; the whole complicated machinery of her body had collapsed. She no longer felt fear. She supposed she wouldn't have felt cold or hunger or pain. No longer herself and not altogether living, she moved in a confused and tragic dream. She knew that she still existed because her eyes could see and her ears could hear. She was alone in a strange, dead world of her own.

Her life was in higher hands now. She took a deep breath, a breath of surrender. Where would she go from here? At the next stop, she would climb from the wagon and . . . what then?

In the clutches of mental prostration and victimized by weariness, Nathalie closed her eyes and slept. She slept soundly, an exhausted, life-giving sleep. The miles bled away, miles that led through a country of vast silence.

When, at length, Nathalie ascended from the deep,

hollow shelter of undisturbed sleep in which for more than six hours she had lain, the day had worn through to dusk and the wagon had stopped. She could hear the sound of water rushing over rocks; voices moved nearer and nearer to her hiding place. Unreasonable panic overtook her, a reaction to the extreme emotions of the day. In her overwrought state, she considered herself full of doom beyond all reality. Each sound struck a blow to her hope of further concealment. Once she suppressed a scream. Her heart beat so rapidly that she breathed in ragged gasps.

"Is this where we will camp tonight, Da?" A child spoke.

"Yes, Jeb. A nice, clear stream flows nearby. And a good time we will have, you and I."

"Will you be glad to get home, Da?"

"Yes, son, I will. Virgie will be missing us, don't you think? I'm anxious to know if Granny Boston is in better health."

"Me, too."

"Let's make a campfire. I'll fetch the matches—"

When the man pushed back the canvas curtain, Nathalie heaved herself upright with a small cry, which she tried with all her might to smother. She had been discovered!

"Why, Jeb, look here. We have an angel riding with us!" the man exclaimed.

"A really angel, Da?"

"I've never seen a better likeness of one."

"Please, sir, I—" Nathalie stared at him searchingly. Who was this person? Her mind somersaulted backward. *Mr. Stan Oliver,* the man she met at the fort. Their eyes touched, and some unspoken message passed between them though Nathalie could not have told what or why the sight of his honest, handsome face left her warm and weak. At once, she knew that Mr. Oliver would protect her, would conceal her, even if it meant his life.

"You are dressed much too lovely for my humble trap," he said gently, "and if my memory fails me not, your name is Miss Thommason. We met on the trail."

"Yes, sir."

"And you have become lost from your caravan, I am to assume?"

"No. That is, I . . . I ran away—from Mr. Whitt."

"You ran away from your husband? I believe Mr. Whitt told me that you were to wed?"

"Oh, no, no! I ran away to escape a marriage to him. I did not know . . . you see, I learned—just in time—that he has other wives. It isn't right. It is adulterous—" She felt herself blushing at talking so candidly to a stranger.

"Indeed, it is wrong. And where are you going, Miss Angel?"

"Miss Angel," the child giggled, and from then on, Nathalie was stuck with the label.

"I . . . I don't know where I am going. Just . . . away. I will find a job—if I can." Tears budded. "Oh, I really don't know what I shall do. I have nothing, no clothing but this wedding dress and my papa's Bible and the doll."

"If you would like to bump along with us, Miss Angel, Virgie will care for you until you can get your bearings about you." His eyes lighted when he smiled. "We've another week of travel, but we've enough grub and tow sacks aplenty for bedding. You are welcome."

"Your . . . Virgie won't mind?"

He chuckled. "Not a whit. She's a sport, that one. Makes the best buttermilk pie on the continent. You'll see."

Jeb had moved to the tail of the wagon. "May I help you down, Miss?" He offered his small hand.

"Why, thank you, sir!" she said, taking the hand as if it were the strongest hand in the world though it would have been quite useless in case of a misstep.

The sound of distant hoofbeats brought Jeb's head up with a jerk. "Da?"

"Sounds as though someone is coming along our trail," Mr. Oliver said, inclining an ear. "And at a rather fast clip."

Nathalie, still clinging to the Bible, pondered her predicament. She was a single girl in the company of a family man and his son. If the rider stopped, Mr. Oliver might be put in a compromising situation, called upon to explain the unusual circumstances of her presence. It could prove baneful, especially if the horseman was an acquaintance.

"If you will excuse me, sir, I will refresh myself at the stream yonder." She was gone before he could reply.

And none too soon. The rider came on at breakneck speed, reining his steed at the campsite as if it were his destination. "I say, Mr. Oliver!" greeted the uninvited guest.

"Erman Whitt! What brings you here at such a frantic pace?" Stan's voice held an element of surprise.

"I am looking for someone, Stan, and I have reason to believe that you know who."

"I?"

"Only an angel rode with us, sir," piped Jeb.

Erman ignored the child. "Don't feign innocence, Stan

Oliver. I know that you kidnapped my bride, Miss Nathalie Thommason. And I will see you hanged for the crime, to be sure."

"I have kidnapped no one, Mr. Whitt. Surely, you are mad."

"The kidnapper could be no one else. You were in Sweet Springs six hours ago, which corresponds perfectly with the disappearance of my espoused. The wedding meal was ready to serve. The cake was prepared. The elder was there. And you took her from the window—"

"I did not take her. I did not know that she was there."

"Hortense said that you took her. She saw you."

"Who is Hortense?"

"Hortense is one of my wives."

"Hortense has defective eyesight—or she is lying."

"I will search your wagon, Stan."

"Help yourself."

Hidden in a thick clump of brush, Nathalie could hear Erman's jerky movements as well as his muttering. "Aha!" he gloated. "Here is a doll. Does your son play with dolls, Stan?"

"The doll is a trifle we picked up along the way. It is something Virgie would like," Stan said without hesitation. His words were true enough, though far from the full explanation. "It proves nothing."

"I don't believe you. Nathalie is somewhere about. I shall wait all night if I must, but I shall find her. And you shall pay dearly."

"Whatever you say, Mr. Whitt. Enjoy your wait. Jeb and I plan to camp here for a while. You are welcome to enjoy our vacation with us."

Nathalie heard the conversation in its entirety. She

hoped that her clothing sufficed for the chill of the evening hours that were becoming frosty around the edges. Erman would surely give up his vigil before long; he was an impatient man and Eleanor, his new toy, awaited him at home.

But Erman could be stubborn, too. He moved close to the campfire to warm his hands.

"I fear you will have to sleep on the ground tonight, sir," Stan mentioned.

"I will do whatever I must," he replied stoically. "But I will not leave until I am convinced that Nathalie is not here."

In the dark of the night, a stealthy figure passed close enough to Nathalie's covert for her to touch. She held her breath. Was it Erman? Would he find her? A coat dropped, almost at her feet. Stan hummed a tune so that she would know it was he.

She wrapped herself in his coat and slept peacefully, dreaming of strong arms about her. When she awoke, horse and rider were gone.

Chapter Nineteen

Stan's Home

So pleasant was the trip that Nathalie wished it might never end. She wished it guiltily but wished it nonetheless. She enjoyed Stan Oliver's company. He laughed a lot, his countenance free from care. She adored his infectious buoyancy of spirit, his even temper, his cheerful conviction that everything worked for the best. The hard stone that pitted in Nathalie's stomach dissolved, and she likened herself to a prisoner suddenly released.

Mr. Oliver insisted that Nathalie sit on the wagon seat with himself and Jeb. "So that you can see where we are going, Miss Thommason," he joked. "No one wants to look back all the time. We must look forward!" A soft breeze from the west, moist and cool, favored them, and it seemed to Nathalie that Stan slowed his pace to make the road stretch longer.

If she tried to worry, the man got between her and her fret. "The good Lord has a plan for you," he encouraged. "He has promised never to leave nor forsake you. Just think of all He has delivered you from already! That should build your faith." When he recited scriptures, he reminded her of Papa.

She found herself confiding in Stan Oliver, sharing bits and pieces of her life, then suffering embarrassment because of her openness, wishing she had said nothing. But he was easy to talk with, an understanding man. She recounted the trip west on the caravan, the trials and triumphs. "I should have listened to my heart about Erman Whitt," she confessed. "Papa wrote me a letter telling me to follow my heart. But I overrode the inner warnings and almost self-destructed. I learned a great lesson."

"You had a wise father, Miss Angel," he said.

"I did," Nathalie agreed. "He left me some solid guide-lines for my life, and I plan to abide by them."

"I wish I could have known him."

Stan described the land to which they were going. "The trees are huge, and a big river runs to the ocean. Everything is large except our village and our houses. They are small. We have a handful of scattered wooden homes, one plank highway and a half dozen dirt streets. That sums us up. But we are never without a pretty smell! My cottage has only one room and a lean-to for sleeping. We're not fancy folk. You will like Virgie."

"I'm sure that I will—if she is anything like you." After the words were spoken, Nathalie scathed herself for say-ing them. Mr. Oliver might misinterpret her intent.

"Virgie and I both have a sense of humor," he grinned. "That's the only way she can stay in the same house with me."

Nathalie, becoming ill at ease, rowed the conversation

back to safer shores. "I hope that I may find employment right away so that I will not be a burden to you."

"Oh, you can find work in Portland, some job befitting a virtuous lady such as yourself. But don't worry about being a burden. You shall not be."

"Tell me about Portland."

"Portland is a large town that is fairly bursting at the seams. Everybody there is as busy as a dog with three cats to chase—and about as confused. Personally, I like the quieter life. But I'm afraid that the city will someday swallow our bit of a village whole."

"I should like to teach school."

"And marry, perhaps?" he teased lightly.

"I will not, sir, until my heart bids me."

"Ah, a bidding heart—"

"I'm sure you . . . understand." It happened again. Their eyes met briefly with a look of comprehension like players familiar with the rules of a great game.

"Oh, quite well, Miss Angel," he responded in the tone of one offering a precious confidence.

They had come to a plank street, and Stan turned the wagon up a dirt road. "Whoa!" he called to the horses, pulling the dray to a stop at the foot of a heavily wooded lot. "We will have to walk from here," he said.

Jeb took Nathalie's hand. "I will lead you," he offered, taking her down a path banked by briars and wild ferns.

The cabin, surrounded on every side by bushes, came into view. It reminded Nathalie of her own cottage in Medford Mill, bringing a wave of homesickness. Lucky Virgie!

"Here we are, Miss Angel," Jeb said proudly. "This is our home."

111

Stan held the door open for Nathalie to enter. "Virgie!" he called. "We have a guest."

There was no answer.

"Virgie must be out back," he said, starting for the back opening. He stopped at the oilcloth-covered table. "Oh, here is a note."

"What did she say, Da?" Jeb pressed.

"She says that Granny Boston is none improved, and she will be there for a while yet." Stan rubbed his chin. "Well, well. This poses a problem for us, Miss Angel. With Virgie gone, I'm afraid you will not be comfortable with me and Jeb. It would not look proper. In Virgie's absence, I mean—"

"No, no, Mr. Oliver. I couldn't stay. Is there a . . . a poorhouse where I might go—?"

"Never!"

"But I haven't any money."

"Westerners are quite hospitable, Miss Angel. I will find you a place to board until you can find a job. Let's see; let me think. I believe Mrs. Wingate, over in the north hem of Portland, takes boarders. You can probably work out your rent. Do you sew or cook or tend children?"

"I will do anything, Mr. Oliver, as long as it is honorable work."

"God takes care of His children, Angel. Somehow, troubles work out. Please sit and let me fetch you a cup of hot tea." He removed the stove's iron lid and struck a fire.

Nathalie's heart didn't want to leave. Ever. But it wasn't right to envy another woman's home. Or husband. Or child.

Jeb came to stand beside her. "I wish you would stay," he said. "Forever. Ma would like you."

Chapter Twenty

Miss Angel

Mrs. Wingate, a stout, sturdily built woman over the hill of forty, had a practiced eye for anyone whom life may have abused. Therefore, she bore immediate empathy for the homeless and penniless Nathalie and clucked about the girl like a mother hen.

"Why, you were stood up at the altar, weren't you, my poor dear?" She gaped at Nathalie's rumpled wedding dress.

"It was I who did the jilting," Nathalie's smile was feeble. "Actually I ran away from a man who wanted to make me his fifth wife."

"Four wives had died already?" Mrs. Wingate gasped. "That is mighty suspicious. I would run, too."

"All of them were alive and well—and living together."

"Oh, one of those kind." Mrs. Wingate set her lips in a hard line. "I've heard stories like that, but I never believed them."

"It is true."

"But how—? Well, that's none of your business, Janet

Wingate." She slapped at her own lips.

"I was innocent, not realizing the travesty until the day of my wedding. One of the other wives let the cat out of the bag. When I found out, I escaped through a window and climbed into the back of Mr. Oliver's cart. That's why I'm here."

Mrs. Wingate threw back her head and laughed. "Oh, what a story! And what did Mary think of this?"

"Mary?"

"Stan calls her Virgie. Her name is Mary Virginia."

"I didn't meet her. She is . . . away. That's why Mr. Oliver brought me to you."

"Oh, oh. Just wait until Mary hears! I've known Mary Virginia all of her life. Though she won't admit to it, she is jealous of Stan."

"She has no reason to be jealous on my account, Ma'am."

"I'm sure that is true. You are pure hearted. But most single women who come west alone are very forward. I can't blame Mary for not trusting them; she is quite fond of Stan and a bit overprotective, I would say. Well, here you are with me, and I've always wanted a daughter. But let's see . . . what shall we do for a garment for you? My gowns would swallow you twice over."

"I can baste a frock in to my size if you have needle and thread."

"Indeed I do."

"But I would not wish to impose on you in any way, Mrs. Wingate. I can dismantle this gown and make it into a day dress."

"You'll do nothing of the sort! You might need that pretty wedding gown here in the West where pure maidens are much sought after. I've some bonny feed sacks in the closet if you can coax them into a covering for your body. Sewing isn't my talent."

"I'm handy with shears. I made my entire wardrobe at home."

Janet Wingate sighed. "And I will be most grateful for another set of hands to knead dough. I run a cafe of sorts for the workingmen. Each meal finds my table full. I hope that you will stay with me for a long, long while."

"I will stay as long as God wills, Mrs. Wingate."

The Wingate house had four separate rooms, which made it quite large in comparison with Stan Oliver's cabin. Mrs. Wingate showed Nathalie to her quarters, a spacious and airy annex. Nathalie's heart lifted. *Here I will earn my living. Here I will find fulfillment. Here I will be at peace.*

But no sooner had she settled in than a restlessness clawed at the lining of her mind. She missed something. Or was it someone? It seemed as if a light had gone out. She picked up the skirt that Mrs. Wingate had brought for her to alter, jabbing at it so forcefully that she pricked her finger with the needle. The moment of physical pain relieved the awful gnawing of emptiness.

A daily ritual began. Nathalie cooked, set the table, and washed dishes. The busier she kept herself, the better she felt. She could not allow her mind the leisure of unleashed thought. Each evening took her to her bed spent, too weary for retrospect or reverie.

But a lengthy stay with Mrs. Wingate was not on the divine map for her life. Before a month had lapsed, before Nathalie had completed her second dress, a letter came for her.

"You have a letter, Nathalie," Mrs. Wingate announced.

Nathalie blanched. "For me? But . . . nobody knows that I am here. That is, except for Mr. Oliver." Her hands shook so that she could hardly fasten the needle into the top of the dress she was designing. Had Erman Whitt found her?

She ripped open the envelope, unfolded the notepaper, and tried to take in the whole of the dispatch in one glance. It was from the local school board, offering her a teaching position in a country school nearby. The salary, the letter informed, would be ten dollars a month with lodging included and a "pounding" of groceries periodically. The previous teacher had relocated, and Nathalie had been recommended to replace her. She was needed immediately. Would she be pleased to reply at once?

How did anyone know? Stan Oliver, of course. He had wasted no time in spreading the word that a new teacher had come to the territory.

"I will take the job," Nathalie said aloud, inflicting upon Mrs. Wingate a spasm of curiosity.

"What did you say, Nathalie?"

"I have been offered a teaching position," she responded.

"For next year?"

"For right now. I will pay you for the bother I have caused you, Mrs. Wingate."

"You have earned your keep, Nathalie, and then some. I've never met a harder worker! You shan't pay me a farthing. You have been a blessing, and we will remain friends. My home is open to you at any time. You can visit on weekends. And I will have my revenge upon Stan Oliver, for I am sure he is the culprit who took you from me! I planned to keep you forever! But of course you must go. Teaching is a high calling, and the children need you."

The transition happened fast. Nathalie rushed her answer back, and by week's end she was taken to her new assignment by a member of the board. To her surprise, her own quilt box sat in the apartment, a small appendage to the schoolhouse. Who had put it there was not a question. How he obtained it was.

"Send for me if you run into trouble," the trustee said. "Not that I think you will. You've come with a glowing recommendation from a man we trust. If you need anything, let us know." He favored Nathalie with a smile of approval and hurried away.

Nathalie looked around. No luxury abode here: only a washstand with an ironstone chamber set, a bunk, a dresser with a cracked mirror, a table, and a chair. Yet suddenly her heart filled with ecstasy. Was the fount of her joy the job or the recommendation?

Rag rugs garnished the rough pine floor. The cabinet was filled with food. *I came west, Papa,* she said, *and I will faithfully fulfill my mission here. And I will keep my promise to you.*

On Monday morning, her nerves sang like a bowstring. She had never stood before a class. Would she be able to plant grains of knowledge in the fertile minds of her students? Was she capable of the task before her? Stan Oliver thought so—and she couldn't disappoint him.

She went early to light the fire in the potbellied stove. Someone had already lit it, the room was warm, and Jeb sat at one of the smaller desks.

"Jeb!" she cried. A stir of fierce joy seized her. "Is this your school?"

"Today it is, Miss Angel. When we learned you'd be teaching here, I traded schools. It is farther, but Da will bring me every day in the wagon. He wants me to have the very best education, and he said you would be the very best teacher."

"But I thought your papa traveled—"

"Not in the wintertime, Miss Angel. He can't get across the passes."

That means Erman Whitt cannot cross the passes either, calculated Nathalie. All facets of the thought brought comfort: Mr. Oliver wouldn't go, Erman Whitt would be blocked, and Jeb would be with her each day.

"I brought my tablet and my pencil," Jeb said. "Where should I sit?"

"I don't know, Jeb. When the others arrive, we will see which places are taken."

Nathalie walked to the window. A range of mountains rose in the distance, summits that bespoke strength. *I will lift up mine eyes unto the hills, from whence cometh my help.* That was one of Papa's favorite Scriptures.

By nine o'clock, the class had assembled, each taking his or her place. The girls sat on one side of the room, the boys on the other. Their eyes appraised her, causing a bout of stage fright. She rapped on the desk for attention, and the room became as hushed as a morgue.

"I am your new teacher," began Nathalie. "Each of you will tell me your name, and I will tell you mine."

"Miss Angel!" piped a voice from the back. "The new boy has done told us!"

And from that day forth, she was Miss Angel.

Chapter Twenty-One

The Writing Assignment

Nathalie began each morning's class with Bible reading and prayer. The first week, her class numbered twelve— the same as the Minor Prophets, the disciples, and the tribes of Israel. Five of her students were girls and seven were boys, leaving many empty desks.

"More will come," offered one of the older boys. "When Miss Pitcock moved, the school shut down. Not everybody has learned that it is open again. I know that Bobby and Sarah and Sam and Joey will come. They hanker for books."

"How many?" Nathalie asked.

"Oh, we're only half here," said a girl with pigtails.

And others did come. They appeared until there were twenty-nine in all, ranging in age from seven to sixteen. Each of them represented a beloved treasure to Nathalie. All the pent energy of her nugatory months found vent in the need she saw benched before her.

Many of the youth lagged in their studies because many

exercises did not hold their interest. Nathalie, merciless in her drive to bring them to their full potential, rewarded them with praise for a lesson well done. She strove to ignite within them a sense of excitement, of discovery. Slowly she led them, not through the musty labyrinth of words and figures, but into a sunlit realm of order and meaning. Sudden glimpses of the magic hidden within the arrangement of words, intoxicating visions of a universe awaiting understanding, became theirs. Language was the vehicle for thought. Grammar was the slave of logic. Diction was a carriage for imagination. Prosaic sentences became the beautiful, beating life of mental labor.

She *could* teach! She *would* teach! She would teach these future leaders to write clean, clear, correct sentences that opened into clean, clear, correct paragraphs. Who could know? Cached within her little group might be a mayor or a governor or a president!

However, the majority of the class was not accustomed to work. When she made assignments, she read complaint on their faces. Yet she valued results more than affection, respect more than popularity. She was impervious to sly infractions or simulated incomprehension. "What is the hardest to master," she instructed her pupils, "offers the most special rewards: rewards such as pride, self-respect, and the gratification of having succeeded. There is no easy way to learn some things really well."

Each evening, Nathalie returned to her room with a sense of deep satisfaction. She loved her students, she loved her work, and she abode steadfastly by the rules she made for herself: Never raise your voice. Never become angry. Never lose patience. And never become derailed from professionalism.

To better understand each of the children, Nathalie assigned a composition on the theme "My Wish" to be due on Friday. She took the papers home with her that weekend to read them.

"I want to be a doctor," wrote one lad. "My baby sister died for want of medical help, and I don't want anybody else's baby sister to die. It hurts too much to lose a baby sister." Remembering the loss of Nan, Nathalie laid aside the paper and wept.

"My wish is to marry a rich man," wrote a twelve-year-old girl, "and have a big drawing room filled with pretty pieces of furniture and a grand piano. But if I can't find a rich man, I want to marry anyway so I will have someone to chop the wood." *Dreams* . . . all girls had dreams. She prayed that this girl's dreams would not be shattered as her own had been.

"I wish I had someone to tell my secret thoughts to," wrote the shyest of her class. "Someone who would not laugh at me." Ridicule, the cruelest of all human interchange. There was none who didn't fear it.

Nathalie saved Jeb's essay until last. "I would like for Miss Angel to live with us and make us happy," he wrote. "Da would be happy if she was there and so would Ma." The page blurred before her. She could hear Stan's full-toned, vibrant voice. She fought the memory, a recall so persuasive it seared like a flatiron. How many hours, how many days had she tried to forget?

Stan Oliver brought his son to school each day and picked him up afterward, but she seldom saw the man. And she was glad. He always arrived early and waited outside so as not to disturb her class. A rear door from the schoolhouse led to her quarters; this she used at the moment of dismissal. Why did she try so doggedly to avoid him?

"Da says you are good, Miss Angel," Jeb whispered one day. "Good all the way through, just plain filled up and overpouring with goodness. That's why he brings me to school here." Nathalie tried to expunge the words from her mind. She didn't want them to affect her, but the untamable things did! For the rest of the day, something hummed in her heart.

Jeb was her favorite pupil though she took care never to betray a hint of preference. The boy often brought too much in his lunch pail—an extra apple, a biscuit with ham, a baked yam or johnnycake—and insisted that Nathalie have it. "Da said to share with Teacher," he would grin, adding a new prick of dolor to Nathalie's spirit, raising guilt in some obscure way. Lately, it took more effort to erase pleasant thoughts of Stan Oliver.

Twice a week, Nathalie found a crock of milk sitting on the outside ledge of her window. She didn't know who set it there, nor did she try to find out. Was she afraid of the truth? Perhaps she was. . . .

The local citizens said that all signs pointed to a hard winter. It began in November. Fog hid the mountain peaks, and snow swirled down the valleys. A stiff wind picked up needles of ice and flung them in a blinding rush through the air. Several times the snowdrifts banked so deeply that the children could not get to the school. But always a stack of logs were placed beside the back door, along with a box of kindling, covered so that Nathalie might have dry wood in wet weather. It had been put there, Nathalie knew, by someone great of heart, someone who needed no thanks, whose courtesy was instinctive in his granite character.

During the holiday break when Nathalie especially suffered the pinch of loneliness, Stan and his son came with a quart of cider, a nut cake, and a gift for her. "Virgie sent the food, and the gift is from Jeb," Stan grinned, a boyish gesture that quickened Nathalie's pulse.

She did not ask them in; it would not be proper. "Thank you," she said, hoping they would leave before the lump in her throat grew quickly enough to choke her.

The gift box contained a book of poetry and an appliquéd dresser scarf with multicolored thread for embroidering its delicate design. She hugged it to herself and cried. Why was she weeping? For sadness? For gladness? For inordinate desire? Or was it for a lost dream?

The long evening hours were filled with the stitching of Jeb's gift and the reading of the poetry from which, ever so often, she could hear a special voice.

Chapter Twenty-Two

The Revival

Winter crawled to its finish. Then came the spring rains and a wonderful sense of newness. Had grass ever been so green, flowers kissed with such lustrous hues?

Papa had been right. The West was Nathalie's place. She'd found her calling. The little she had to give, she was giving it unreservedly. The young minds of her students were growing, developing. For this cause was she created. Her scholars could accomplish goals that she would never reach: Doctors, lawyers, parsons, builders, *wives.* . . .

With her nose against the windowpane, she viewed the faraway peaks. "Your eyes will blur to find with sharp surprise . . ." Where had she read that? The rest of the lines tantalizingly eluded her. Find what? She could not remember. But for an instant, she felt the sharp surprise, as if she stood on the edge of some wonderful discovery, something lovely, entrancing, unexpected. "Thank you, Papa. Thank you, God," she said. "I am blessed."

Five days a week, she approached her schoolroom

with eager anticipation. She would have been pleased to run the classes day in and day out, year in and year out with no breaks. Already she dreaded the Easter holidays and a week of idleness.

Then a letter came from the school board. It was customary during the spring recess, the letter informed, to open the schoolhouse for a gospel meeting. A second letter followed, a letter from Mrs. Wingate suggesting that Nathalie stay with her and offer her apartment to the preacher. She expressed her desire to spend some time with Nathalie again, saying that it would be a nice diversion for both of them. Nathalie welcomed the arrangement. With her embroider work finished—and the poems memorized—she had nothing to occupy the vacuous hours threatened by Easter's intermission.

"Of course, we will go to meeting each night," Janet Wingate told Nathalie when she arrived. "Everyone for miles around goes to meeting. People will be hanging out the windows."

"Does the community choose a different preacher each year?" Nathalie asked.

"That depends upon availability. Stan recommended this one. He met him on his rounds somewhere. His name is Danby. Brother Danby. Jeb calls him 'Brother Dandy.' They say he is a fine preacher though he doesn't spare the sinner."

Brother Danby. Could it be?

"I will be eager to hear the preacher."

Nathalie wore her nicest dress, fashioning her hair in an eye-pleasing coil. Mrs. Wingate lent her a bone comb for her chignon. The mirror threw back a becoming reflection, igniting a nameless flame in Nathalie's spirit.

Would the Oliver family be there? Would she meet Mrs. Oliver?

Desks had been removed and log benches arranged inside the school building. When Nathalie and Mrs. Wingate arrived, the seats were already filling. Nathalie followed Janet, who took a seat—heaven forbid!—directly behind Stan Oliver.

"Miss Thommason!" Stan turned to take her hand in greeting, prompting a blush in her face.

Jeb beamed with delight. "Ma, this is Teacher."

"Miss Angel! I am Mary Oliver, though Stan calls me Virgie," the woman greeted. "I am pleased to meet you, I'm sure. Jeb sings your praises morning, noon, and night, and the hours in between!" Her teeth were even and white, and when she smiled her whole face underwent a transformation. If not quite beautiful, it certainly became fascinating as an alert sensitivity harmonized all its planes and angles into an enchanting revelation of the intelligence and spirit that lay behind it. *I will never,* thought Nathalie, *forget that face. I would expect a man such as Stan Oliver to choose just such a companion for himself.* She swatted at a gnat of envy that landed on her consciousness and hoped she killed it.

Brother Danby entered, more gaunt than Nathalie remembered, his face chiseled, his chin pointed to accentuate a large nose and high, brushy brows. His hair, of no definite color, had thinned in the months since she had seen him. His tired gray eyes, spanning the gathering, found Nathalie and flickered with recognition. Now and again those eyes returned to hers and were instantly averted. Nathalie managed to observe him indirectly.

What hymns were rendered or what testimonies given,

Nathalie could not have told. She fought with unknown fiends. The closeness of Stan Oliver suffocated her. He was so near she could reach out and touch him, and she suffered a temptation to do just that. Oh, wicked heart!

She was glad for the sermon, glad for the ring of Brother Danby's challenging voice, glad for the fire in his eyes that kindled awed respect in the listeners. He seemed to press to get to the worst of his indictments as soon as possible. Presumptuous souls, he warned, who planned to walk on the pavements of heaven must not try to build a tower of Babel to get there. At the end of his discourse, he directed his remarks to the poor obstinate sinners who could not see that pain was inserted into their lives for their own good.

Nathalie, possessed of an inner fester, was convinced that she was, indeed, a poor obstinate sinner. The message was given by God to Brother Danby for her own salvation. Deep in her mind she found the seed she had not yet allowed to germinate. She must extract the sin of covetousness if she would join her mama and papa in the great beyond. And oh, how disappointed Papa would be if she didn't make it! She crowded to the mourner's bench with the other seekers and asked for forgiveness.

After the service, Brother Danby made his way to her. "Miss Thommason," he said, forgetting to release her hand, "thank you for allowing me to lodge in your room. It is most commodious. And I am blessed to see that you did not wed the gentleman on the wagon train. Certainly it was not God's divine will. I prayed many prayers for your deliverance." As he spoke, light shone around him as though the setting sun had bathed him with the same suffused glory with which it touched the mountains.

"Thank you for your prayers, Brother Danby. God was indeed gracious to me."

"You shall be back tomorrow evening?"

"I would not miss a service."

Chapter Twenty-Three

The Preacher

"We will prepare a meal and invite Brother Danby to eat with us," Janet Wingate insisted. "It will be an honor to feed the preacher. His sermons are speaking to our hearts."

"That is gracious of you, Mrs. Wingate," concurred Nathalie. "I will be glad to help in any way that I can. I make a tasty gooseberry cobbler."

"Perfect!" she cheered. "We shall host him on the morrow if he will consent to bless us with his presence. I'll ask this evening. Set some bread, will you?"

Brother Danby accepted the invitation with obvious delight and, surprisingly, Nathalie found herself at ease in his company. He reminded her of Papa. Few men possessed the clarity, the purity, and the simplicity of genuine Christianity that flowed from this godly man. What made him so remarkable? His integrity was bedded on courage, but it was more than bravery. It was honest but more than honesty. When his humanity showed through the cracks of his holiness, Nathalie loved him the more.

She was pleased when he asked for a second helping of her pie. "This is the best pie I have ever tasted," he avowed. "You are an excellent cook, Miss Thommason." But coffee he spurned, a fact Nathalie had noted on the trail. She supposed he listed it as the devil's brew.

After the meal, Mrs. Wingate bade Nathalie entertain their guest while she cleared the table. Apparently, this pleased the preacher, and he took a chair so that he might see Nathalie's face as they talked.

"Now, if I am not being presumptuous, Miss Thommason, may I ask how you were able to forego your commitment to Mr. Whitt?"

"My commitment?"

"The marriage commitment."

"I made no commitment, sir. The plan and the idea were his alone."

"He told me that you wished to be his bride."

"Mr. Whitt is not a truthful man. I did not wish to be his wife. That is, not until the last. And even then, I was unaware of his duplicity."

"His duplicity?"

"He already had three wives."

"No!"

"Yes, sir. I learned on my wedding day that I would share his affections with four others. For on the day he took me, he planned to take another also. But God was merciful to me and delivered me."

"Oh, then that is the burden that I felt for you. I knew that evil lurked somewhere. I beseeched God until that burden lifted. But tell me, how did you manage to escape?

People of that sect are very manipulative and controlling. And very powerful."

"I fled through a window, found a supply cart, and hid there. The cart . . . came here."

"Was it, by chance, the wagon of Stan Oliver?"

Why did the mention of that name tighten Nathalie's chest? "Yes, sir. He and his young son were returning from a trip."

"Oh, Stan Oliver is a good egg. I knew it when I met him back at the fort. One can just tell. Uprightness cannot hide itself, but neither can unrighteousness. Stan told me about himself and his family. No one could love a son more than Stan loves little Jeb. The child is truly a gift of God. I surely must go and visit them while I am here. They have invited me.

"But tell me, Miss Thommason, do you enjoy teaching school? It is a most honorable calling. My pappy was a schoolmaster, and I have the highest estimate of the position."

"Oh, sir, I do like to teach! I want my life to count for something. I have nobody, you see, but me—" Nathalie halted, flustered.

Brother Danby rescued her from the quagmire. "Would you like a pianoforte there, Miss Thommason?"

"I would, but I could never afford that!" Nathalie returned.

"I have an aged aunt, grave ready," he said, "who would be glad to see her instrument go to a worthy cause. I'll put your name in the hat for the instrument."

"Oh, dear Brother Danby, that would be too wondrous!"

The preacher's eyes showed tenderness. "But Miss

Thommason, you will not always want to teach, I'm thinking. The lifestyle is too lonely, too isolated. Look at me. I travel through the world alone, with no family and few friends. It is not God's plan for a beautiful woman like you to forfeit a husband and children in the name of education."

"I . . . that is . . . there is no one—"

"Ah, there will be. There will be. You will be a joyous bride. And I, Miss Thommason, will be happy to marry you myself. Oh, I couldn't have committed myself to a ceremony on the trail. But now . . . now everything is different."

Nathalie was astonished. *Papa's rules . . . don't marry a man too old.* How old must the preacher be? At least fifty? With enough birthdays to be her grandfather? She loved Brother Danby but not . . . not that way.

Her mind reeled with shock. Brother Danby was proposing to her? She had overheard the conversation between him and Erman Whitt. He said he could not take a wife because of his nomadic life. He couldn't support a family. Had his circumstances changed? Had he come into money?

"How old are you, Brother Danby?" Nathalie asked suddenly, at once mortified that she'd broached the personal subject.

He actually smiled, his faded eyes holding but the ashes of human desire, starved and buried in the graveyard of sacrifice. "I'm fifty-four, Miss Thommason. I have spent and been spent for my Master. I've never married anyone before, but my ministry needs a good marriage to round it out, a marriage that will last a lifetime. I am old enough to do that deed, don't you think?"

"Y—yes. But I made my father a promise, you see. He set some rules—about age—and I cannot break them."

"I see. It is honorable of you to respect your father's wishes and keep your promise to him. But when you are ready to marry, just send for me, and I shall be happy to marry you. And in the meantime, we will keep in touch. I'll have the piano sent."

Chapter Twenty-Four

Intruder

On the last night of Brother Danby's stay in Nathalie's apartment, a dreadful event happened. The annex was broken into, causing the preacher a period of terrible angst. It happened in the dark of the night, he told Stan, somewhere past midnight.

He heard a noise, a crash. The door was pushed in and heavy footfalls tramped to the bedside. Before he could speak, a familiar voice sliced through the shadows.

"Aha! I found you, Nathalie Thommason," the intruder said, "and I shall have you at last. You thought that you would get away from me, didn't you? You made it look as though you had been kidnapped, slipping away in the wedding dress. But no one gives Erman Whitt the slip. You will be sorry that you tried. You should have known that I would locate you when you sent Stan Oliver for the quilt box. Hortense cannot keep a secret. You weren't hard to find. I knew you'd be teaching school somewhere nearby."

The man held up a lantern, and when he saw that the figure on the bed was a man and not Nathalie, he fled. Brother Danby, his righteous indignation awakened, jumped from the bed and pursued Erman, his long johns gleaming white in the night. Being much longer limbed than Erman, he outdistanced him in a short space.

He caught Erman by the collar. "What are you doing here, Erman Whitt?" he growled. "Speak up."

"It is a mistake!" bawled Erman. "Let me go."

"It is no mistake. With your own mouth, you are condemned. You came for Miss Thommason. I am a witness; I heard you say so. You came to kidnap her. I can have you arrested this very night. And I shall, unless I find sufficient reason to release you."

"Please, sir. I will do anything you say. Anything! You see, the lady was supposed to become my wife—"

"She does not wish to be your wife. She never wished to marry you. You deceived her. You hid the fact from her that you had other wives. You misled her. That is akin to perjury, and I can have you arrested for that, too.

"I have talked with Miss Thommason this very week. She has . . . other interests. I see now why I could not join the two of you as you wished on the trail. It would not have been holy matrimony, and God could not sanction it. How can a man be 'one flesh' with five people? Tell me that.

"I told Miss Thommason this week that I will be gladsome to join her in holy matrimony with her husband when the day of her wedding comes. God will give her an upright man, and I shall perform the ceremony if she will allow it."

Brother Danby still held Erman by the collar.

"I didn't know there was anyone else in her life, sir, really I didn't. I was only trying to make a good life for an unfortunate girl. She'd lost her home, her father, everything. I felt sorry for her; I wanted to help her."

"And you came here tonight wanting to help her?"

"I tell you what, sir: If you will let me go and not report this incident, I will take my leave and will never bother Miss Thommason again. It is a gentleman's promise, sir. Shake."

Brother Danby did not extend his hand. "Get out of here, Erman! Go before I sully my ministry by hurting you!" He gave the man a helpful boost. "And if you ever come again, I will see you brought before the judge and convicted as a criminal."

Erman slunk away, and the preacher went back to bed. Into the hours of the morning he prayed. "Now I know why you sent me here, God. I was disappointed that more sinners didn't come to you, but my coming has saved Miss Thommason's body and soul. We love Miss Thommason, God. I love her. Jeb loves her. And Stan loves her. She's made her father some promises. Help her to keep those promises. Amen."

With that, Brother Danby fell asleep.

Chapter Twenty-Five

A Sick Child

The close of the revival relieved Nathalie. After her visit with Brother Danby at Mrs. Wingate's house, she avoided contact with him. Such a humble man as he should suffer no more disappointments in life, but she could not in good faith marry him. Even if she wished to do so, her promise to her father would prohibit the union. Age disqualified the preacher.

And, too, she was glad to return to her apartment, back to the school routine that would occupy her mind, taking her thoughts from the emotions the preacher had stirred, the longing for strong arms to hold her, for a shoulder to cry on. Work was her panacea.

A new shipment of books and maps came. She had not ordered them, but regardless of the benefactor, she was elated. None of her pupils, she supposed, had ever seen books with fresh backs and no pages missing. The up-to-date supplies called for a special celebration. She made a teacake for each child.

After the Easter break, Jeb returned to school, but he wasn't his cheerful self. He sat quietly, his concentration aborted. Nathalie worried about him. Then, with the passage of a week, he didn't attend at all.

Nathalie sifted through her memory. Had she offended the child? Had she said something amiss? What could have occasioned his withdrawal from school?

The classroom was a dismal place without Jeb's smile. Nathalie walked in a blur of grief. Had it been any other member of the class, she would have visited or written to learn the problem, but she declined to go to the home of Stan and Mary Oliver. Such a trip was not feasible anyway, she told herself, conversely knowing that Mrs. Wingate would take her anywhere she wished to go.

Two weeks inched by. Two miserable, gloomy weeks. Then, at the close of the school session on a Friday, Nathalie looked up to see a man's form fill the doorway. She stiffened.

"Miss Thommason?" He smiled, a slow, calm smile, and without cognizant thought Nathalie backed up a step.

"You have come for Jeb's books?" she asked Stan Oliver.

"No," he answered, "I've come to ask a favor of you."

"Yes?"

"Jeb is very ill. He is calling for you. Will you pay my son a visit?"

"I will come tomorrow," Nathalie stalled. "I'm sure that Mrs. Wingate will bring me."

Stan shook his head and a lock of dark hair fell over his forehead. "I promised Jeb that I would bring you today. Can a man disappoint a child, Miss Angel?"

"A promise is a promise," Nathalie recited as if by rote. She'd made a promise to her own father, and shouldn't she help Stan Oliver keep his?

"You might want to take a satchel of clothes," Stan was saying, "in case you need to stay."

"I couldn't possibly stay overnight," she objected.

"I wouldn't burden you, but he is so very ill . . . and . . . and I am afraid . . . "

Nathalie locked the schoolhouse and climbed into the wagon with Stan, the wagon that had brought them special closeness last year. They rode in silence while a breeze played with Stan's heavy hair, lifting it from his face. From the corner of her eye, Nathalie saw his glance bent upon her when he thought himself unobserved.

"Your son . . . how long has he been sick?" she inquired.

"He hasn't been himself since the Easter break, Miss Angel. His fever is high. Virgie is afraid he has the scourge, and that is deadly. But if anyone can help his spirits, you can."

"I will try."

Nathalie wasn't prepared for the frailty of Jeb. He had lost weight, weight he didn't have to spare before the illness. He lay inert on the horsehair sofa, covered with a heavy quilt. His small frame shook with a wracking chill. Mary motioned Nathalie to his side.

Nathalie cradled the limp hand in her own. "Jeb," she said softly, "it's Miss Angel."

"Miss Angel?" The boy tried to smile and didn't quite succeed. "I've been plagued that you would miss me at school."

"I have missed you, Jeb. Oh, how I have missed you!

143

Without you, I have been sad." Oblivious now to everything around her, her heart cried to the sick child. "You will get better for Miss Angel? Just for me?"

Hearing a sniffle, she looked up, and Stan was hurrying from the room.

"Jeb's attachment to you turns Stan's heart to mush," Mary explained. "He has a soft spot for the child, you see. You would think that Jeb was his own flesh and blood."

"He . . . isn't?"

"No, though Stan has had him all his life."

"He isn't your son?"

"No, Miss Thommason. I am not married."

"You . . . aren't married? But I thought you were Mr. Oliver's wife—"

Mary gave a half laugh. "Oh, won't Stan think that a hoot! I am his sister. I help him with Jeb, keeping Jeb when he travels. He called me over three days ago when Jeb . . . took a turn for the worse. Of course, I love Jeb, too. He's like my own, I've kept him so much. But why did you think—?" Comprehension lit her face. "It is because I came to the meeting with Stan, isn't it? He came by and gave me a ride each night. I stay with Granny Boston. She's our mother's mother. Our mother is dead."

Facts were hailing too fast, facts Nathalie wanted, craved. A sudden pulse of joy rose in her, and the future donned enchanting colors. Stan Oliver wasn't married! Her quirky mind dredged up the story of the three bears with their too hot, too cold, and just right porridge. Erman was married, Brother Danby was too old, but Stan Oliver was just right for a husband. Surely he would fit perfectly into the promise she had made to Papa.

"Tell me how Mr. Oliver got Jeb," she heard herself saying.

"Please call my brother Stan. Mr. Oliver sounds so old, and Stan is but twenty-five."

Twenty-five. That will fit nicely into Papa's rules.

"Stan married Jeb's mother before Jeb was born. Jeb's father was drowned at sea."

Nathalie's heart plunged, leaving her sick inside. Her hope died. And the death of a hope genders no less grief than a physical death. *Papa's rules . . . take to yourself a man who has not given his body or soul to another woman.* The rule banished Stan Oliver from her life forever.

"Stan, brave, unselfish Stan was only eighteen years old when he married Gail. He had been left with the house here, Mama's house, and Gail was left homeless. So he married her, and then she died—"

"Miss Angel," Jeb called. "I will work hard to catch up. Aunt Ma, my pillow is wet and the cover is too warm."

Mary laid a hand on the child's clammy forehead. "Thanks be to God," she gloried. "The fever is breaking."

When Stan came back into the room, Nathalie glanced up, her face rigid. "Jeb's fever is gone, Mr. Oliver. He will be better soon. Please take me home. I have . . . things to do."

She dared not look at him on the way to her apartment; the pain was too sharp, the anguish too great. When he helped her from the wagon, he took her hand and kissed it. "Thank you, sweet Angel," he said. "You are wonderful."

In the warm intimacy of his glance, she caught the thrill of love's embrace. The sentiment left her startled— and afraid, for he had found her heart unguarded.

145

She removed her hand and dashed into the building without looking back.

Chapter Twenty-Six

Determination

Nathalie sat numbly, raked with a torn heart, gripped by a paralysis of confusion. She saw nothing, heard nothing. *What is happening to me?* she asked herself, feeling the scald of tears tracing a path to her chin. *I love Stan Oliver, that's what. Oh, why must I love someone that I cannot have?*

"True love comes without warning if the heart is ready," her father's letter said. It had come. "Let your heart regard neither wealth nor poverty in your decision." Stan Oliver had little of the world's goods, but Nathalie didn't care a shard. "Above all, choose a man who loves God and country, who is in accord with your upbringing and godly principles." That shoe fit Stan. Never had she felt more in accord with another person on earth, even Papa. But one rule stood between her and unbounded joy: Stan had been married.

"I love Stan Oliver so much that I ache inside from loving him," she cried, "and yet I cannot marry him because of my promise to Papa. How could Papa's instructions be so contradictory? He tells me to follow my heart. If I follow my heart, I will lay it at Stan Oliver's feet. But he has given himself to another, a forbidden act in Papa's statutes. Which do I heed: my heart or Papa's instructions? What can I do with a love so strong?"

Letters came for Nathalie, unsigned missives. Mrs. Wingate brought them to her. Nathalie was certain that she knew the benefactor. She detected the hand of Brother Danby in them, and the knowledge gave her reason for further distress. Poor Brother Danby. If ever anyone deserved a good wife, he did. But his age aside, she loved Stan Oliver. What a paradox!

In the first letter, her admirer hinted of his love for her. He had no right to ask for her hand, he wrote, for he had little to offer. But did he have a chance? She did not respond. A fear of hurting the old minister stayed her pen.

Other letters followed, but after the first, Nathalie had no inclination to open them. She would go to her grave a spinster before she would break an innocent man's heart with pretense. Yearning for Stan, she would be unjust to marry anyone else. And, with the same sense of loyalty, she would die brokenhearted before she would violate her promise to her deceased father. She and Brother Danby would share a life of bitter sacrifice, though each in separate worlds. His remorse would soon end; hers was just beginning.

How Nathalie managed her classes to the end of the term, she never knew. She ate little, tossed in her sleep, tormented by dreams of Stan's hair blowing in the wind. She counted the days until school dismissed for the summer while cringing at the prospect of the long, lonely intermission. How would she survive the eternity?

She was standing at the window when the piano came, borne of four men. And with it, the thoughtful Brother Danby had sent a self-teaching course. Now she would have something to occupy her summer hours! She would learn to play and play well. Her soul would find its outlet in music.

She directed the movers to install the instrument in the schoolroom. "Brother Danby said to tell you that the instrument is a gift to you, not to the school," said one of the workers as he turned to leave. "And he hopes that you will enjoy it."

"Oh, I shall! Thank you!" She ran her fingers over the ivories, anxious to acquaint herself with each note. It was a lovely instrument, well kept and richly finished. God had seen her suffering and had sent this bequest as a balm for her wounded spirit.

Just when the fangs of the cruel thought struck her, she did not know, but with its black venom a deadly poison of misgiving spread through the arteries of her soul. Of course! Brother Danby had sent the piano so that she might learn its melody, its notes to be an asset to his ministry. So that she might sing and play and woo sinners with her voice and her music. How could she have failed to see the motive behind his generous offer?

And now, knowing why he sent the gift, could she take advantage of his hopes by going along with his plan? She would return the piano, she resolved, if only she knew where to send it. The joy of having it was gone; its music would be sour to her ears, acid to her heart.

He meant well, poor dear. But she must tell him she could not accept the gift on his terms. There was no need to begin the lessons. She closed the lid on the instrument and didn't open it again.

Summer blazed forth in its avalanche of color: the dark redwoods, silver aspens, gold hickories, and bronze oak trunks. But Nathalie hardly noticed. She could not respond to the beauty about her, for there was no pleasure within.

She read her papa's letter over and over, underscoring every word in her heart, determined to keep her promise to him at whatever cost to her desires and dreams.

A promise was a promise.

Chapter Twenty-Seven

Dark Days

Each night's sleep came only with exhaustion. Questions tumbled over questions, never finding answers. Why did she make the promise to Papa? Would he look down from heaven and know if she broke that vow? Her nerves were raw, her emotions spent.

School was out, the children gone. The piano sat idly, and the hurt within Nathalie had settled to a dull, aching throb. Life had no meaning.

At length, weariness claimed her, fogging her brain. Hammers pounded in her head and the room whirled as she stumbled to her bed. What cared she if she never arose?

The sheet was heavy, dreadfully heavy. The weight seemed to hold her down, crushing her. Her mouth felt dry, her tongue swollen. Water . . . if she could have a drink . . . but her body was too weak to go for a cup. Everything drifted away but pain.

Mrs. Wingate bent over her. "Am I sick?" Nathalie murmured, trying to open her eyes.

"You have a fever, but you will pull through. We are praying." A spoon touched her lips, and she let the cool liquid dribble down her throat. It felt good. Day slipped into night, and night into day. Again and again. Mrs. Wingate changed her gown, bathed her with a wonderfully damp rag.

Someone else was talking. She sounded like Maggie. "Yes, we bought land next to the Oliver place. I want Nathalie to see our new daughter. We named her Jan." It was surely all a dream.

Another voice, another time. A man. Was it Papa? *Remember the promise, Nathalie. Yes, Papa, I remember. I'm keeping the promise.* Hours. Day. More hours. More days.

Sounds, sounds that made no sense. What did the words mean? Was that Brother Danby praying? Keep praying, Brother Danby. Yes, he would pray. He would pray until she could hear again, see again. He would pray until she was alive again. But she couldn't marry him. He was too old. Too old . . .

And there was little Jeb. Or was it a dream? She'd like to take him in her arms and hug him. She'd tell him how smart he was, how she enjoyed having him in her class, and how handsome his dad was. They were running around the schoolhouse, laughing. Holding hands. Then she was playing the piano and singing at Brother Danby's revival meeting. She was playing a song about heaven. But Brother Danby was too old for the promise, remember?

She was rushing toward Stan Oliver, her arms open wide. But no! A wall stood between them. A wall with "The Promise" scrawled across it. They couldn't cross the wall to each other. She was crying, pleading with Papa to take the wall down. *Please, Papa!*

And here came the children, all twenty-nine of them. Hi, Miss Angel, this is Elizabeth. We want you to get well. Here is my homework, Miss Angel. This is Carl. Remember me? I'm the one who wants to be a doctor. If I were a doctor, I would make you well. On and on they marched. Will you teach us again next year, Miss Angel? She could feel their love, and she wanted to return it.

Cowering in the background was Erman Whitt. Go away, Erman. Go back to your wives. You will never win now because Brother Danby prayed. You cannot win against God. Go back to Odene and Grace and Hortense and Eleanor. I am free.

From a very long distance, someone called her name. She was too tired to answer. Answering was too much effort. Again and again the voice pled, just out of her reach. Someone needed her. . . .

She must lift her eyelids! The familiar voice was gentle, coaxing. He was whispering in her ear: "Nathalie, don't leave us, dear. Can you hear me, Angel? I love you more than life itself. *I love you!*"

The words melted into a prayer. "God, save my precious one. We need her, God, Jeb and I." The voice cracked. "You promised her to me, God, away back at the fort. Remember?"

Nathalie tried to lift her head, but it was too heavy.

"I'm not worthy of her, Lord," the voice prayed on. "I can't offer her life's luxuries. I'm a poor man. Do with my Angel . . . as You will." The voice stopped.

It was Stan's voice. He needed her. He loved her. But he didn't meet Papa's requirements. She would have to tell him. And, oh, it would be hard.

Chapter Twenty-Eight

Keeping the Promise

Nathalie's eyelids fluttered open to find Stan sitting beside her bed, holding her hand. Tears pooled in his eyes. "Oh, you are awake! My darling, I . . . I thought I had lost you!"

"I . . . I can't—"

"You can't what, dear?"

"I can't marry you. I made a promise to Papa that I . . . I wouldn't marry anyone who had given himself to another woman—"

"And that's why you didn't answer my letters?"

"Your letters?"

"Didn't you get them?"

"No."

"I sent them by Janet Wingate. She said she brought them to you."

"Oh—the letters. I . . . I didn't know they were from you. I thought they were from Brother Danby. I'll . . . I'll read them . . . someday. But it's all the same. I promised

Papa, and a promise is a promise."

"What promise did you make to your papa, Angel?"

"I promised Papa that I wouldn't marry anyone . . . anyone who'd given his love, his body, to another woman."

"Please let me explain my past, Nathalie. Gail lost her husband just days before Jeb was born. She was ten years older than I was. They were our neighbors, and her husband was a dear friend of mine. She was left with no one to provide for her. I was eighteen, able-bodied, and had the home place. I couldn't let a woman soon to be delivered of a child suffer deprivation. We decided it wouldn't look right for her to stay with me without the benefit of legality. So I married her to give her a home. Then, shortly after she brought Jeb into the world, she died. Her death was partly due to the grief for her husband, I'm sure. She loved him devotedly.

"I never knew her as a wife, Angel. I never loved her as a wife. So really, I've had no wife, you see. We were married in name only—"

"Oh, Stan, my love. Then . . . then—" Would her heart rupture from the joy that filled it? "Then I can marry you and still keep my promise to Papa, can't I?"

"You can. Will you be my wife, Miss Angel? My first wife, my last wife, and my only wife?"

"Yes, oh, yes, Stan, my love—"

"But, you see, I made a promise, too, sweetheart. I promised Gail that I would rear Jeb for her, as my own son. And I love him. Will that pose a problem for you?"

"Not at all! I have Papa's rules memorized word for word. Jeb is an 'orphan indeed' and Papa would have no problems with that. I will love you both forever and always! And I hope that Brother Danby won't be too disappointed."

"Disappointed? Why, he will be beside himself!"

"But he wanted to marry me."

"And he shall. He'll be delighted to do just that. He told me a long time ago that he wanted to be the one to hear your vows, to perform the ceremony for us."

The truth seeped in slowly. Brother Danby meant . . . he meant he wanted to marry her to Stan Oliver! Why, he understood God's plan all the time! It was she who had misunderstood.

"And so I promised Brother Danby that he would be our preacher for the big day. I made that promise by faith," Stan was saying. "And a promise is a promise, you know."

"I know." She brought his hand to her lips and held it there.

"And we've some new neighbors who can't wait to see you, old friends of yours."

"Of mine?"

"Albert and Maggie Pascoe and baby Jan, who is eager to meet you."

"Hold me, Stan, my beloved. I think my heart might explode!"

Nathalie closed her eyes, ready for his first kiss, her heart singing with the happiness of this day . . . and all the days that lay ahead.

I kept my promise to you, Papa.

Rest in peace.